Unruly Catholic Women Writers

Unruly Catholic Women Writers

Creative Responses to Catholicism

Edited by

Jeana DelRosso, Leigh Eicke, and Ana Kothe

excelsior editions
State University of New York Press
Albany, New York

Excelsior Editions is an imprint of State University of New York Press

For information, contact State University of New York Press, Albany, NY
www.sunypress.edu

Production by Eileen Nizer
Marketing by Kate McDonnell

Library of Congress Cataloging-in-Publication Data

Unruly Catholic women writers : creative responses to Catholicism /
    edited by Jeana DelRosso, Leigh Eicke, and Ana Kothe.
        pages cm
    Includes bibliographical references.
    Summary: "A literary anthology exploring contemporary Catholic
women's experiences"—Provided by publisher.
    ISBN 978-1-4384-4830-5 (pbk. : alk. paper)
    ISBN 978-1-4384-4873-2 (hardcover: alk. paper)
    1. American literature—Catholic authors. 2. Catholic women—
Literary collections. 3. American literature—Women authors.
I. DelRosso, Jeana, editor of compilation.

PS508.C54U57 2013
810.8'09222—dc23   2012045440

10 9 8 7 6 5 4 3 2 1

In Sisterhood

Contents

Part One: The Joyful Mysteries

Part Two: The Sorrowful Mysteries

Part Three: The Glorious Mysteries

Acknowledgments and Permissions

The editors would like to thank the following individuals and presses for allowing us to republish some of the pieces we have included in this volume:

Lauren K. Alleyne originally published "Holy Thursday: The Passion" in *Imaginatio et Ratio: A Journal of Theology and the Arts* 1:1 (2012): 32.

Lauren K. Alleyne originally published "Resolution" in *Temba Tupu! Africana Women's Poetic Self-Portrait*, ed. Nagueyalti Warren, Trenton, NJ: Africa World Press, 2005.

Lauren K. Alleyne originally published "Sunday Morning in a Foreign Country" in *Small Axe: A Caribbean Journal of Criticism,* a division of Duke University Press (July 2011).

Lauren K. Alleyne originally published "The Taste of Apples" in *Gathering Ground*, ed. Toi Derricotte and Cornelius Eady, Ann Arbor: University of Michigan Press, 2006.

Lauren K. Alleyne originally published "Fear and Trembling" in *The 2River View* 10:4 (Summer 2006).

Suzanne Camino originally published "Age of Reason" in *On the Edge,* a publication of the Detroit Catholic Worker (Summer 2007): 13.

Ava Cipri originally published "Excuse Me for This Sister Mary" in *New Zoo Poetry Review* 11 (2008): 11.

Sarah Colona is publishing "Moth Song" and "Our Lady of the Library" through Gold Wake Press (forthcoming).

Sheila Hassell Hughes originally published "Interior Castle" in "A Woman's Soul is Her Castle: Place and Space in St. Teresa's 'Interior Castle'" in *Literature and Theology* 11:4 (1997): 376–84.

Pat Montley presented "Confessional" as a scene from *Acts of Contrition* at the Edinburgh Fringe Festival, 2012.

Mary Rice's poems are copyrighted © 2012 by the Estate of Mary Rice.

Natasha Sajé originally published "Anathema" in the *New Ohio Review* 6 (Fall 2009).

Leonore Wilson originally published "Invisible Nature" in *TRIV-IA: Voices of Feminism* 7 (Sept. 2008).

I have never written a single thing of my own volition, but rather only in response to the pleadings and commands of others; so much so that I recall having written nothing at my own pleasure save a trifling thing they call the Dream.

—*Sor Juana Inés de la Cruz*[1]

Introduction

Mysteries of the Faithful, Dreams of the Future

Catholicism is mystery. Or so Flannery O'Connor, perhaps the best-known American Catholic woman writer, suggests in her foundational text, *Mystery and Manners*. "Christian dogma," she writes, "is about the only thing left in the world that surely guards and respects mystery" (178).[2] Such a statement proves difficult to dispute, as mysteries abound in the Catholic tradition, and many facets of Catholicism must be taken on faith. For example, the doctrine of the Holy Trinity, which posits that three persons—God the Father, God the Son, and God the Holy Spirit—exist as one being, can only be understood through belief, not logic. The doctrine of papal infallibility, or the belief that the pope can speak through divine revelation, asserts that he is, in these instances, incapable of error and that his pronouncements cannot be questioned. And the ritual of the Catholic mass is largely based on mystery, particularly the transubstantiation, in which wafer and wine are quite literally transformed, Catholics believe, into the blood and body of Jesus. Theoretically, then, mystery is central to much Catholic teaching.

Practically, however, the mysteries of the church can serve to create problems for some of its constituents, particularly women. The rules and regulations of Rome often limit women's abilities within the church community and our mobilities within the church hierarchy, preventing Catholic women from achieving full autonomy and from accessing the highest leadership positions in the church system. Indeed, women bump their heads against the glass ceiling of the church hierarchy before they move very far up at all, as women are denied ordination to the priesthood and thus to entrance into the positions of bishops, cardinals, pope. Female Catholics are also thereby prevented access to one of the seven sacraments. These policies become yet another of the Catholic mysteries, which we are told to accept unquestioned, on faith.

We the editors of this volume have taken the Catholic doctrine of mystery and used it as a way of thinking through women's roles in the church, particularly as women enact unruliness in the face of such unquestionable faith. Our first anthology, *The Catholic Church and Unruly Women Writers: Critical Essays*, published by Palgrave Macmillan in 2007, covers varied critical perspectives on both canonical and lesser-known Catholic women writers, all focusing on unruliness in what is commonly thought of as a restrictive site of writing for women: Catholicism. Geared toward scholars of literary criticism and women's studies, this collection addresses issues of gender and religion that remain central to the lives of many women living in the world today.

Following the same spirit of inquiry regarding the extent to which the Roman Catholic Church enables or restricts female unruliness, we now offer a second volume, this time of creative pieces—short stories, poems, personal essays, dramatic works—on the topic of unruly Catholic women. As demonstrated by our first volume, Flannery O'Connor is but one unruly woman; in women's writings on Catholicism, unruliness abounds.

In keeping with the sense of Catholic mystery, we have thus organized our volume around the mysteries of church doctrine: the Joyful Mysteries, the Sorrowful Mysteries, and the Glorious Mysteries of the rosary. In the Roman Catholic tradition, praying the rosary is a form of meditation—often silent and individual, but occasionally public and communal. The rosary demonstrates a form of devotion to the Blessed Virgin Mary; each of the five decades of the rosary involves praying one Our Father, ten Hail Marys, and one Glory Be. Praying these decades, the devout Catholic meditates on the Mysteries, which invoke a meditation on certain

New Testament events in the life of Mary and her son, Jesus. So the Joyful Mysteries evoke prayers on the Annunciation, the Visitation, the Nativity, the Presentation of Jesus at the Temple, and the Finding of the Child Jesus in the Temple. The Sorrowful Mysteries include the Agony in the Garden, the Scourging at the Pillar, the Crowning with Thorns, the Carrying of the Cross, and the Crucifixion. And the Glorious Mysteries consist of the Resurrection, the Ascension, the Descent of the Holy Spirit, the Assumption of Mary, and the Coronation of Mary.[3]

The rosary is also a form of prayer most often associated with women. Many of us with Catholic upbringings remember our mothers and our grandmothers, rosaries wound about their fingers, whispering their prayers in the evening as they counted off their beads, then blessing themselves with the crucifix when finished. Such devotion to Mary is often central to Catholic women's faith.[4] Many women continue to envision Mary as an unruly woman, choosing to become the mother of God, embracing her fate, and standing strong as she watches the murder of her only son. Her inner thoughts on the path her life took remain, of course, a mystery to us.[5]

So we have approached the mysteries of the rosary, and of this first woman of the New Testament, with an eye for the various paths that women take today and the various decisions we make in our lives. Our reading of the Joyful Mysteries continues to invoke motherhood, childbearing, and childrearing, but the writers in this section of our anthology may view those particular mysteries differently, or may make some alternative choices altogether. Our version of the Sorrowful Mysteries still includes stories about pain and death, but we look at other forms of pain that women experience both in and through the church, such as alienation from the church community through divorce or sexuality. And our Glorious Mysteries explore the ways in which Catholic sacrament and ritual, combined with female unruliness, offer new visions for a Catholic future for women. Indeed, many of these stories demonstrate women's willingness, even eagerness, to embrace their Catholic faith, despite the obstacles. As contributor Colleen Shaddox points out, "To be raised Catholic and switch denominations is a lot like giving up Haagen-Dazs for broccoli. You miss the richness, even if you know it's bad for you."

Our contributors come from a wide range of backgrounds and experiences, and their unruliness varies in both form and content. While the genres in this volume range from poetry to nonfiction prose, from fiction to drama, the writers themselves span generations and geography, race and ethnicity, sexuality and socioeconomic status; and their writings represent all stages of life, from birth through childhood and adolescence, from young adulthood to middle age and death. They also represent a wide array of attitudes toward and positions on the religion they address: some are practicing Catholics while others are clearly reticent, retired, or recovering; some are entering the church while others have left it far behind; some defend the mystery and rituals of the religion while others declaim and defame it. Finally, some are authors with considerable records of publication and prizes; others are just emerging into the discipline, finding their way through words as they find their way through a Catholicism that may either welcome or reject them.

We the editors believe that, with the 2012 Vatican censorship of American nuns, there will be a resurgence of interest in literature that addresses the relationship between Catholicism and women. And, indeed, while our contributors also vary greatly in their treatment of the religious sisters—finding them sometimes liberating, sometimes oppressing of other women—we the editors support our fellow women in their feminist struggles against an out-of-touch hierarchy whose priorities seem to be deeply skewed, as they attack nuns who do the real work of Christ and yet defend priests who abuse and molest our children. We hope that our volume may make some small contribution to a growing awakening and awareness of social justice and equality in the Roman Catholic Church, as well as to a Catholic populace currently struggling with issues of loyalty and activism, voice and voicelessness, intellect and faith.

The creative responses to Catholicism found in the following pages speak to us as readers but also to each other, forming a community of women not often found within the confines of the institutional church. Their collective perspective offers us new ways of probing and, perhaps, solving some of the mysteries the church sets for us, Catholics and non-Catholics alike. As O'Connor writes, "The Catholic writer, insofar as he has the mind of the Church, will feel life from the standpoint of the central Christian mystery: that it has, for all its horror, been found by God to be worth dying for" (146).[6] The unruly Catholic woman writer finds similar mysteries in the church; but, as the following works prove, she most often finds her life to be worth living for.

Notes

1. *The Answer/La Respuesta*. Trans. and ed. Electa Arenal and Amanda Powell. New York: The Feminist Press, 1994. 97.

2. Flannery O'Connor. "Catholic Novelists and Their Readers." *Mystery and Manners: Occasional Prose*. Sel. and ed. Sally and Robert Fitzgerald. 1969. 170–85.

3. In 2002, Pope John Paul II created a new set of mysteries, the Luminous Mysteries, which include the Baptism of Jesus in the Jordan, the Wedding at Cana, Jesus's Proclamation of the Kingdom of God, the Transfiguration, and the Institution of the Eucharist.

4. A good amount of recent scholarship in the area of the medieval worship of Mary has been undertaken. See, for example: Stephen Shoemaker, "Epiphanius of Salamis, the Kollyridians, and the Early Dormition Narratives: The Cult of the Virgin in the Fourth Century." *Journal of Early Christian Studies* 16:3 (2008): 371–401; Susan Carter, "The Diby *Mary Magdalen*: Constructing the *Apostola Apostolorum*." *Studies in Philology* 106:4 (2009): 402–19; and Jeanette Favrot Peterson, "Creating the Virgin of Guadalupe: The Cloth, The Artist and Sources in Sixteenth-Century New Spain." *The Americas* 61:4 (2005): 571–610.

5. More recent scholarship on Mary ranges from theoretical approaches, such as Julia Kristeva's classical essay, "Stabat Mater"; to books, such as Wendy Wright's *Warrior and Peacemaker: Faces of Our Lady in Los Angeles*, Santa Barbara, CA: Santa Barbara Mission Archive-Library, 2008; to scholarly articles such as Mary Hunt's "Women-Church: Feminist Concept, Religious Commitment, Women's Movement." *Journal of Feminist Studies in Religion* 25:1 (2009): 85–98.

6. Flannery O'Connor. "The Church and the Fiction Writer." *Mystery and Manners: Occasional Prose*, op. cit., 144–53.

Part One

The Joyful Mysteries

the first joyful mystery

Susanne Dutton

although he was a virgin
Mary loved God,
followed him home,
rang his bell
and ran away,
left silly notes
and sat like a kitten
in his courtyard,
mewing.
finally throwing her teenaged
kneesy-ankled-elbowedness
with such a crack
against his door
that he left his ease
to let her in,
to let her twine blue ribbons
through his will,
to say "yes" to Mary.

Praying Twice

Liz Dolan

Her fingers fluttering
like sparrows' wings,
Sister Benvenuta taps
the lectern which holds her up.
Under the soft folds of
her linen gown, her candle-wick body
flickers, her black veil ballast.

Over and over pale notes
wash the rough-hewn walls
of the chapel until she leavens them.
Like Chanticleer she cocks her head
at a sour sound. Her iron will makes
plainsong rise like baked bread:
slowly, dark-grained, oval-shaped, and crusty.

My Soul Sisters—or, How the Nuns of my Childhood Inspired a Feisty Feminist

Renée Bondy

I have known quite a few nuns in my day—a women's historian, I gather their oral histories as part of my work. I've met so many sisters: old and young, pious and irreverent, devout and lapsed; nuns who pray and nuns who curse; nuns in traditional habits and nuns in Levis. If you are a Catholic woman of a certain age, perhaps you've met them, too. And whether you are more familiar with Sister Mary Perfect, or her wicked counterpart Nunzilla, or the scores of sisters who fit somewhere in between these stereotypes, they have very likely shaped you, challenged you, and made you the woman you are today.

I teach in a Women's Studies program at a small Canadian university and, semester after semester, I learn more from my students and colleagues than one could ever hope to glean from a textbook. To be in an environment where women encourage, inspire, and move one another to action is a gift, one with which I have often been blessed throughout my forty years.

I grew up at what was, arguably, a revolutionary period in the history of the Catholic Church, in the years immediately following the Second Vatican Council. The late sixties and seventies were, for some, a hopeful time, years when the promise of change seemed remarkably sincere, when lay-folks felt empowered to speak out, to shape the Church of the future. Things were changing, seemingly for the better; the throwing open of windows and doors promised by John XXIII was, indeed, letting in a breath of fresh air.

By the seventies, Catholic schools in my part of the world, southern Ontario, Canada, were decidedly unlike the Catholic schools of my parents' generation. I had heard stories from my father, uncles, and aunts about the sisters who taught them: severe, pinched women in long black habits whose harsh punishments bordered on the sadistic. Though I had never met these sisters, I feared them, much as a child might fear the dark, or an unseen monster under her bed.

From what I could determine as a young girl, Catholic schools had come a long way, and the most marked difference was in the teaching staff. Where previously nuns had staffed and administered schools, now lay people, both women and men, were the majority. And the sisters who remained were certainly not those of the habit-wearing, rosary-toting, ruler-wielding variety. The sisters of my school years were middle-aged women, maybe ten years or so from retirement, who wore navy polyester skirts and groovy wooden crosses on leather lanyards. Their sensible shoes were so unfashionable as to be almost chic, and their once obligatory short haircuts were on par with the then-trendy pixies and shags.

Looking back, I recall Sister Monika as my first teacher-crush. I was nine, maybe ten years old, and Sister M was our music teacher. She wore an acoustic guitar on a beaded macramé strap, and she looked for all the world like Joan Baez. We loved her. I say "we" because *all* the students loved Sister M. Few of us had any real vocal talent, and some of us were altogether hopeless when it came to music, but we all joined in and belted out the popular Christian folk tunes of the day. Sometimes, once Sister M was warmed up, she would leave the folk mass standards behind and launch into Pete Seeger's "Where Have All the Flowers Gone?" or even Dylan's "Blowin' in the Wind." Though young, we felt that we were, in our own small way, a part of the social movements of the era, united with students across North America who sought equality for the marginalized, marched for peace, and challenged authority.

In the tenth grade, Sister Bernadette taught our religion class. As I recall, the assigned textbook examined themes in the Old Testament, but although Sister Bernie had good intentions of guiding us through the curriculum, it didn't take much encouragement to get her off topic. She had just returned from ten years' missionary work in Lesotho, Africa, and had countless stories to tell about her adventures. I didn't, even for a second, want to be a missionary, but Sister Bernie's compassion and zeal were contagious, and I know I wasn't the only student who walked away from her classes ready to take on the world. If a grey-haired, five-foot-tall nun could travel thousands of miles from home and confront the challenges of poverty and injustice, then maybe I could change the world, too.

Sister M and Sister Bernie were just two of the many sisters who influenced me as a young woman. There were many others along the way—youth group leaders, professors, writers, and counsellors—and each, in her own fashion, raised my consciousness and set me on the path to feminism. I'm not so sure that many of them would have used the "f-word" to describe themselves, but they were among the most engaged feminists I've known in my lifetime. Through them, I discovered folk music and developed a passion for social justice. I learned that I didn't need a man or children to define me, and that makeup and stylish shoes were nowhere near as important as a head held high, a strong voice, and the confidence to stand my ground. They inspired me to study theology, education, and women's history, and to make my own way in the academy. These sisters not only modeled good teaching practice, but they also engaged in what bell hooks calls "teaching to transgress," and instilled in me the belief that education is the key to authentic freedom.

Most importantly, I learned from these sisters about the role of women's communities as sources of support and empowerment. Over the years, I've placed less trust in patriarchal institutions, such as the Church, and more in the transformative power of women-together. While I'm not sure that the sisters who taught the young women of my generation would have predicted our widespread mistrust and ultimate rejection of the Church, I suspect that many do not disavow us. We are, after all, their legacy.

Jerusalem Road

Mary Rice

Sisters came here, in the old days—
nuns, that is, when there were nuns
in some numbers.

When they stopped being nuns in that old way—
black-garbed, white-wimpled,
constrained by yards of fabric and rules—
girls stopped joining the orders
and many left. But

in the old days, when there were vocations,
nuns came here in the summer, to this house
by the sea, for vacation.

Jerusalem Road was the destination, winding
along a rocky coast in earthly imitation of their
divine mandate.

Kneeling at the altar rail, they saw a solid wall,
but everywhere else the sea—out windows,
through the porch's balustrade, below the promontory.
With waves endlessly calling, gulls circling,
sky arching over all.

There were walls then, around the grounds,
but the way to the sea was open. And they walked here
in robes too heavy to be much stirred
by the wind, but with eyes lifted up, for once,
to the open sky.

Where I First Met God

Lacey Louwagie

When I was a small child, I thought the priest at our local parish was God. (Little did I know the Catholic Church would later try to sell me on a very similar idea: that the priest was somehow a more valid "stand-in" for Jesus than anyone else—especially a woman. By that time, I wasn't buying it.) Perhaps I came to believe the priest was God because when I whined about going to church, Mom always said that God gave us so much; the least we could do was see Him once a week. The priest was ancient—as surely God must be!—and despite the way he stooped when he walked and mumbled when he talked, he had a kindly face and disposition. When I look back, I feel amazed that I believed that was *really* God standing at the altar and yet still found the service a bore!

Although both my parents were raised Catholic, my mom was the only one in her family who continued to practice as an adult. The Catholic Church was something of a novelty to my cousins on my mom's side. Once, taking a walk with an older cousin, we stopped at the Catholic church in her town. The doors were open, so we went inside. I marveled at the statues, the balcony, the paintings, and the beauty that was both familiar and new at the same time. We both knelt for some perfunctory prayers. I pointed toward the altar and said, "That's where God stands."

She raised an eyebrow. "You mean, the priest?"

"No, I mean God."

She gestured at the altar. "The *priest* stands up there."

"In *our* church, it's God."

She chuckled. "I'm pretty sure it's the priest."

I was embarrassed that my older, cooler cousin found this amusing. I never mistook the priest for God again—much to the annoyance of many in the Catholic hierarchy, I'm sure!

By the time I was ten, my parish had probably voted me "least likely to remain Catholic." I was a thorn in my teachers' sides, constantly demanding better reasons why women couldn't be ordained and editing my workbooks to use gender-inclusive language. I read the edited version when it was my turn to read aloud. After one class in which I'd changed about a million "he's" to "s/he's," a friend and partner in dissent declared with me that, as soon as we were adults, we were going to be "anything but Catholic."

But by the time I was thirteen, the Catholic Church had become the most stable force in my life. My dad had gone back to school, and my mom had started working outside the home for the first time. I was suffering bullying at school and caring for my younger sister at home. Perhaps the worst changes of all were those happening within my own body. Desperate to return to the comparative purity and simplicity of childhood, I sought that purity and simplicity in the Church. The Church provided a structure lacking everywhere else and offered a false sense of control. I began bargaining with God, and Catholicism provided so many bargaining tools! *I'll pray a whole rosary every night if You let me not get my period during school; I'll prostrate myself and pray from now until I hear the car in the driveway, if You'll make sure my parents get home safely; I will obey the rules of the Church, I won't complain about going to Mass, I will stop resenting and questioning and making fun of the priest when he sings if You can make my life make sense again.*

It wasn't all about bargaining, though. I started to feel the real spiritual comfort of Catholicism—the tangibility of my grandmother's red rosary beads slipping through my fingers, the stiffness in my knees after kneeling through the Eucharistic prayer, the

Host gently dissolving on my tongue, the predictable rhythm of the Litany of Saints—and of course, Mary. Catholicism gave me Mary when I was angry with a male God; it was Mary I prayed to when my menstrual cramps doubled me over with pain or when the sticky blood between my legs just wouldn't stop coming. My prayer was simple: "Mary, help me. *You* understand."

Perhaps it was because of Catholicism that my developing sexuality was a barely realized whisper in my adolescence. What had been a childhood fascination with sex quickly turned into a shameful secret under my religious education teachers' instruction. Sex was so fraught with guilt and distress that I gladly embraced the Church's teaching about abstinence—best not to have to deal with it at all! Although my sexual education had included a definition of the word *gay*, I understood implicitly that there were no gay people where I lived. Gay was something that happened far away.

And so, because every person in my whole world expected that I would grow to love boys and men, I expected it, too. Meeting those expectations came naturally enough; my first crushes were on male teachers, and then on boys in my class. I wasn't consciously aware of any same-sex attraction except that I ached under the homophobic social norms that made it taboo to touch my best friend. We rode the same bus, and after she got off, I often spent the remainder of the ride trying not to think about how nice it would be if she could just put her head on my shoulder. Thoughts like this raised a panic within me: *Ohmygod does this mean I'm gay?* I dealt with this terrifying question in two ways. First, I replaced the image of my best friend in my mind with whoever was the least onerous boy in my class. See, that would feel nice, too, right? *Right*. Good. Not gay. Second, I'd imagine having sex with a woman—because being gay was really about wanting to have sex with women, right? The thought of having sex with a woman didn't appeal to me, either. I never considered the fact that having sex with *anyone* at age thirteen wasn't appealing. All I knew was that the crisis was averted. I loved my best friend, but I wasn't gay.

The deal should have been sealed when I was sixteen and fell in love with Drew, a man I cantored with at church. My love for

Drew was wrapped up in my love for Catholicism, until I couldn't really separate the two. I loved going to church because it meant I would stand beside him for an hour and that he would take my hand during the "Our Father" and smile at me first during the Sign of Peace. The smell of the paper in the missalettes was the scent of Drew; the Eucharistic Host dissolving on my tongue was the hope for his kiss. Love letters to God and to Drew filled my journal. I asked God whether I was using Catholicism to get close to Drew, or whether God was using Drew to bring me closer to Him.

But then I had the dream: I was "messing around" with another woman. She had dark black curls and glowing tan skin; I knew nothing about her except that she was beautiful, and that I wanted her. I awoke terrified. This was it, I thought. I really was gay, and my life was over. I had left high school early to start college, so I was at least outside the environment that had taught me that being gay might be the very worst thing I could be. Even so, I pushed the possibility away as hard as I could. I looked away from the posters around campus during gay pride week, left the living room when TV news reported on teachers being fired for being gay, skimmed but never, *ever* read articles about Ellen DeGeneres coming out. Despite my best efforts, the reality that homosexuality existed confronted me everywhere I went. I wished I could pretend that it didn't exist; if it didn't exist, then it couldn't be happening to me.

I was still in love with Drew, but somehow I thought a single homoerotic desire had the power to eradicate every attraction I'd ever felt for males. When I watched movies, I would obsess over the female and male leads—which one did I *really* think was more attractive? I did the same with the men and women in my poetry class. There was a boy who sat in front of me with curly blond hair, wire-frame glasses, broad shoulders, and an intellectual air. I found him attractive, didn't I? Phew, I must be straight. But that boy didn't make the girl in the same class go away—the one with the red hair so vibrant that it was almost maroon, the one who wore bright yellow tights under her shorts and wrote poems comparing seedless watermelon to abortion. *She* was the one I'd noticed on the first day of class.

Finally, I confronted the reality that, somehow, both of these attractions *did* exist within me. I *was* truly attracted to men . . . and to women. I sat alone in the stairwell outside my bedroom, my head held in my hands, when the thought entered my consciousness for the first time: maybe I was bisexual. As soon as I'd named it, a homophobic solution came on its heels: I would just decide not to pursue my attraction to women. Ironically, this is pretty much exactly what the Catholic Church tells me to do.

But neither Catholicism nor Christianity figured into my fear of being gay. I certainly didn't fear what God would think. No, my fear came from knowing I'd have to keep this secret or risk being ostracized by my community. I knew what the Catholic Church's stance was; long before I thought it applied to me, I looked up homosexuality in the Catechism, and I'd heard plenty of Christian preachers blast their opinions about it. But none of it took root. Even when I was most susceptible to the clear-cut answers mainstream Christianity and Catholicism provided—especially regarding sex—they never had any authority with me when it came to homosexuality. I think of St. Augustine's reference to "the law that is written in men's [all] hearts and cannot be erased no matter how sinful they are." The law God wrote on my heart was one of love and acceptance. And I simply knew that, on this matter, mainstream Christianity was wrong.

I thought I'd arrived at a prudent solution: I could inwardly acknowledge who I really was while also pursuing only love that I could declare publicly, only love that didn't entail the risk of being cast out of my community. But the solution must not have been too great after all, because I fell into the worst depression of my life.

God blessed me with chronic migraines. It didn't *feel* like a blessing when I spent most of my teenage years curled up on the couch, my eyes closed against the pain, holding perfectly still to keep from vomiting. But in a rural community where people are still expected to "pull themselves up by their bootstraps" when they're struggling with mental illness, those migraines were my ticket to help. After a long summer of unsuccessful medications, I got a prescription for the antidepressant Elavil. It cut my migraines down from one-a-day to one or two a month. More importantly, it saved me from my depression.

Without the depression's fog over my life, I didn't worry about sexual orientation throughout the remainder of college. I read books with lesbian main characters without feeling afraid to identify with them. I considered myself "about 85 percent straight," but had accepted that sexuality existed on a continuum. I didn't dwell on occasional attractions toward other women. I kept in touch with Drew and had a brief Internet romance with another man, but otherwise made it through college free of romantic entanglements. My most compelling relationships were the ones I had with my female friends.

After college, I moved to Duluth for an internship. I loved the city but didn't know a single soul within it. That's when I started realizing how much other people's expectations and assumptions affected my self-perception. When there were no family or friends reflecting back their understanding of "who Lacey is," I began to feel set adrift, anchored by nothing, perhaps at risk of fading away entirely. It was terrifying.

After nearly a year there, I started taking guitar lessons from Jenny, a woman who was a few years older than me. I still hadn't formed emotional attachments to anyone nearby, and I thought I would lose it if I saw one more warm smile or embrace that wasn't for me. But because of the lessons, being alone wasn't such a heavy burden anymore: it gave me the opportunity to practice and experiment—an experimentation that soon went beyond my music. I listened to tapes of our lessons when I practiced and when I fell asleep at night. I started attending Jenny's gigs, and I couldn't take my eyes off her. Butterflies gathered in my stomach whenever I stood outside her door, waiting for the student before me to finish. One night, driving home from one of her performances, the realization of what it all meant flooded over me: I had a crush on Jenny. And I wasn't afraid. I was elated. She was in a relationship with a man, and I knew nothing would come of my attraction. But it felt *so good* to step into my whole self at last.

After that night, at the age of twenty-two, I started openly identifying as bisexual. I caught up on my gay reading and film, sported rainbows, and became an activist for equality. Later that year, when I met Jayme's ocean-blue eyes for the first time at a party, I knew exactly what it meant. I was totally ready. If I had loved Drew because of Catholicism, I loved Jayme because she was everything else. She was Tibetan prayer flags, karma, and hands dirty from gardening; she was walking barefooted through autumn leaves and the taste of rose petals. I fell harder than I'd ever fallen for anyone. I wrote her love letters, too—but this time, I sent them. Thoughts about how my family, hometown, or the rest of society would react were barely a blip on my radar. The culture's scorn would be a small price to pay for the chance to be with Jayme.

But even as I'd finally come home to my sexuality, I hadn't found a spiritual home after more than a year of "church shopping." When I first moved, I'd visited churches and denominations that were more liberal than Catholicism, knowing that my values were out of line with many "official" Church teachings. But even churches where I was aligned with the values didn't feel like home. I missed the Crucifix and the Eucharist. But although they had depictions of Jesus on the altar, it was hard for me to find Him anyplace else in one unwelcoming, conservative Catholic parish after another. Finally, while attending a work retreat on the far side of town, I got lost and ended up outside the only local Catholic church I'd never attended. Wondering whether there was even a point to it anymore, I checked it out the following weekend. When the priest gave a homily about his own struggle with depression and the social stigma surrounding it, I knew I'd found my church home at last.

And although Jayme and I didn't work out as a couple, we retained a deep friendship that continues to enrich my life. Last year, I took her to church with me. It felt good to have these two parts of my life converge at last. As I drove us home, she said, "The service was nice." Then she paused, and continued, "But doesn't it bother you that you have to say you aren't worthy?"

Lord, I am not worthy to receive You, but only say the word and I shall be healed.

I said quickly, "Well, it's about humility." But after my initial defensive reaction, I let her question sink in. I admitted, "Yeah, I guess it sort of does bother me."

For how many times had the feeling of being unworthy weighed upon my shoulders? It began with sermons about why women couldn't be priests and continued with the Church's resistance to gender-inclusive language. It was in the official Church doctrine that called homosexual acts "intrinsically disordered," with no acknowledgment of the deep love that could be manifested in those acts. It was in the papal decree that men who had "homosexual tendencies" should not enter the priesthood and should be weeded out when suspected—side by side with prayers about the priest shortage! It was in pamphlets scattered at Catholic events about "what the Church says about same-sex marriage," and petitions at the entrance of the church in support of the "Defense of Marriage Act." It was in the way my feet dragged as I climbed the church steps, wondering why I still did this Sunday after Sunday. I understood the message coming from the hierarchy: they didn't really want an unrepentant feminist and openly bisexual woman in their midst. A priest once told me, "It would be better if everyone who doesn't agree with all the Church's teachings would leave. It would result in a smaller Church, but a purer one."

I wonder what Jesus would say about this "purer" Church. I remember that Jesus, too, worked within a failing system for social justice. Despite the priests who had tried to convince me that women couldn't be priests *because Jesus was a man*, I'd begun to notice something they never mentioned. Jesus's body might have been a man's, but the example he set was a woman's. Like a woman, he gathered children on His lap when no one else had time for them, and like a woman He refused to respond to violence with violence. Like a woman, His life was one of thankless service to others. Jesus was a paradigm of androgyny who, like me, loved without distinction for sex or gender.

So I continue to climb those steps every Sunday, because I know I am not alone in my struggle for a more just Church. Being Catholic is so much a part of my life and my history that

I've accepted that it's unchangeable—just like being bisexual is unchangeable. I love both parts of me. And the more I love and accept the person God created me to be, the more I love all of God's people . . . and the more I love God. I know now that the priest at the altar isn't God, but the Catholic Church was where I first met God, nonetheless. And that is not something from which I can turn easily away.

Age of Reason

Suzanne Camino

(for Sr. Gerry Sellman)

Two days past her first communion,
the white dress
a puddle of shiny organza on the floor,
she wants to know
why we never see any women priests
at church, not even one.

Because they're not allowed, baby.
No women allowed.
That's why.

I watch the truth seep in like slow poison
until she squints up at me,

"WHAT?!"

Her voice is so strong.

Shout it again, wise child.
Shout it until the force of your disbelief
makes deaf men hear.

Shout it out loud, bright girl
until they let you whisper
in the center of the sanctuary,
arms upraised and face upturned,

Behold the Lamb of God,
who takes away the sins of the world.

Behold, lambie mine,
he will take away this sin.

Where justice begins
there is a word,
and the word is from God,
and the word is

"WHAT?!"

Come Jesus,
free your eight-year-old girls.
Only say the word and we shall be healed,
we shall all be healed.

Uniforms Optional

Leah Cano

The light above my head was glaring. My eyes were fixed on a small spot on the ceiling as I allowed my thoughts to drift. The silence was soothing as I half closed my lids. It wasn't at all what I was expecting. I knew young hands were sketching, eyes analyzing every line of my fifty-four-year-old body. They were scrutinizing everything: the scar across my abdomen, the misshapen curve of my left breast. I felt a strand of hair lying across my neck and I remembered that I was absolutely *naked*. I had nothing on, but I was strangely at peace.

When I asked about the modeling, the woman said there was a need for a model for a figure drawing class . . . a NUDE model. As she took down information, she asked me what kind of work I did. I said I was an elementary school teacher. I confess, I held my breath, half expecting her to retort, "What? An ELEMENTARY school teacher? Well, how can you DO this?" But she merely asked if I could come in at ten on Tuesday morning. "Yes," I heard myself say, feeling my stomach in my throat as I hung up the phone.

My mother is an artist.

At an early age, I was exposed to art workbooks with illustrations of nudes in various, provocative poses. Though I attended Catholic school and nudity was tantamount to a flirtation with the fires of hell, I knew from an early age that this form of nudity was somehow separate from the other.

My mother had wanted to be a fashion illustrator before marrying my father. She explained to me once that in order to know how a skirt hem would fall, how a blouse would skim the top of the hips, one needed to know about the muscles, the bone, the construction of the human body under it. This made perfect sense to me. This was indeed a different kind of nudity. It was art.

Once my younger cousin came across one of my books for illustrating nudes, shocked at the fact that I would have one of these "dirty" magazines in my possession. Clearly pornographic in her opinion, she ran to inform my mother who simply said, "Yes, I know." This squelched any anticipation of reprimand upon me by my mother, which totally perplexed my cousin that day.

If there was one thing that Catholic school and art appreciation were at odds about, it was the concept of nudity. In school I was taught that any kind of nudity past potty-training age was a sin, whereas in art, it was not only acceptable, it was beautiful.

Magazines, radio, and television taught us girls that when it came to the beauty of the human body, any hint of plumpness was grotesque (the only exception being, of course, if you happened to be Marilyn Monroe, in which case you could be regarded as "curvy").

In college many years later, as I was studying the form of the Renaissance female body, the shadows under the ample breasts, the full hips, and the fleshy, round shoulders, the term that pleased me the most was "Rubenesque." Somehow, I saw these women as *real* women, totally opposite to the more popular fashionable body shape of the time, which resembled a living bicycle.

However, like many young girls, I bought into the belief that the thinner one was, the better. I hid my body at all costs. It was what the nuns called "modesty," but it taught me something else. It taught me to be ashamed of my body because it didn't match what I was being told was beautiful. I would never be thin. I had my grandmother and my father, among others, to thank for this. I would never be able to wear those clothes designed for thin bodies.

Walking down the hallway of the art school before the class, I saw a large painting of a reclining nude. She looked to be about three hundred pounds in weight and had what I could only describe as an expression of outright smugness on her face . . . as though she knew only those with wisdom could see what she had taken half a lifetime to learn—that she *was* beautiful. I don't know who that woman was, but she gave me courage to show these students what great artists like Michelangelo, Gauguin, and Rivera had always known. Women like us who hold the weight of years within our hearts, who have suffered the scars of operations that have permitted us to return to the land of the living, who have harbored the seed of life within our loins, have earned new sight. Our mere existence and the lessons we've endured over the years mingled with joy and sorrow are what make us beautiful. We are still here. We have survived.

When I disrobed I imagined myself removing the Catholic schoolgirl uniform that constricted not only my body but also my mind with the belief that a woman should always hide away her body in modesty (or shame). It slid off my back like melted butter that lay in puddles at my feet. My true self was revealed at last, like a butterfly emerging from a long worthless cocoon.

I had the power to stand there in perfect imperfection because of the lesson life taught me: beauty comes from within and radiates outward through the body no matter its shape, size, or number of scars. After all, in the end, we are all naked.

I pulled my robe on during one of the breaks and wandered around the room barefooted, looking at the varied work the artists had produced. The girls were shy, not able to look at me directly, and blushed quite easily, while the boys became very nervous, sweating profusely as I stood near their easels.

When the class was over and the students were leaving, I dressed again in a small room. Coming out into the large, empty studio, I drifted from easel to easel looking at the nearly completed works. The woman in each sketch had small, mismatched breasts that spilled onto ample hips, dappled with emerging cellulite. They were gracious enough not to outline the varicose veins, I noticed.

Sitting in the car, I thought about that woman in the sketches. There was something about seeing yourself through the eyes of an artist or, in my case, many artists. I wasn't sure what it was, but I decided that the model was missing something other than clothes.

I had nearly given up figuring out what it was exactly, when I heard myself laughing out loud as I pulled out of the parking lot. Merging into the flow of traffic, I sighed with the realization that what she was finally missing . . . was a uniform.

Sunday Morning In A Foreign Country

Lauren K. Alleyne

Here the drums do not sound hosanna.
The spirit moves politely, ignites nothing
but the longing for home. And I ponder
this calling to church, that building
of brick and bond and breaking; wonder
how in spite of the world, its vast suffering,
we can reckon with our own blessings,
our stubborn, complicated luck—praise it.
Perhaps I have seen too many miracles
to think they're not worth asking for.
Perhaps faith is in the longing for thickness,
in the evidence of our seen and unseen selves.
So I go; greet the pale strangers beside me
with Christ-love; listen to the gospel unfold
its demanding promise of love: Above all,
God, neighbor. I will kneel and ask forgiveness
for what I have done, what I have failed to do.
I will remember my dead. I will eat the flesh,
drink the blood, cool in its safe gold chalice;
accept as grace the small salvation of song.

Wool Skirts

Martha Marinara

I am thinking as I tug at my skirt hem, trying in vain to cover my thighs, that any story—especially a story about my body—cannot exist outside culture or outside of the stories we tell about sexuality and gender. Footprints are made by real feet, but it is their impressions that we read. I am still stuck in the "good girl/ slut" dichotomy that I grew up with, and I can only be "the good girl" or the "slut" in the fictions I tell about my body. However attuned one is to the difference between reality and fiction, there isn't as a big a gap as we would like. And no place safe to hide. Telling stories is how we learn who we are, how we discover the many ways—joyful, sorrowful, and glorious—to manifest a self. Telling stories about our lives is how we devise the complexity of our familial identity as it merges and clashes with the identities already determined by our culture. In intricate tapestries we weave threads from our histories and watch our narratives unfold in bits and pieces. Perversely, fictions are fabricated, embroidered on top of tapestry's truth. Without the knots of yarn, strongly twisted in the warp of some authenticity, fiction unravels and reveals the truth more fully than our life stories' hints and ruptures and silences.

My own fiction unraveled quite early, unraveled as I pulled apart the hem of my plaid wool uniform skirt, the wool that covered my thighs too warmly in fall and spring, barely warm enough in winter. The scent of drying wool steamed the classrooms of my grammar school all winter and mixed with the smells of chalk and pencil shavings and lavender soap and the freshly ironed linen scent of the nuns who dominated my first grade world.

Consistently bored in first grade, already capable of reading and writing and so able to daydream with impunity, I picked at my skirt hem so I wouldn't stare at Sister Julie. In November of my sixth year, I was aware for the first time that if she smiled at me, my cheeks would warm and redden and I'd feel like I wet my panties. So I pulled apart the wool skirt that marked my fictive identity, although it would be many years before the narrative of my life, already decided before I was born, would blessedly unravel. Knowing the whole while my mother would be angry at having to repair the hem of my skirt, I pulled at the threads and rolled the broken evergreen bits into little pill-shaped balls that I furtively stuffed inside my desk like some domestic contraband.

The uniforms made us identical in Christ's love, but the colors were how we told each other apart—green plaid for St. Rita's, maroon for St. Nicholas's, brown for Sacred Heart, and blue for St. Mary's. I grew up in St. Rita's parish, a Catholic schoolgirl, an identity imbricated, inebriated in prayer, fasting, self-sacrifice, and constant head-bowing, ring-kissing humility. But I was also Irish, a chance of fate that I believed saved me from losing my soul altogether. For juxtaposed with the mystery of The Holy Trinity was the magic of dancing faerie rings; the little people were real, benign and adorable as Baby Jesus, and a rainbow symbolized God's covenant complete with pots of gold for those who believed in leprechauns. And there was a wealth of poetry from my grandfather and piano music from my grandmother. I thought the litany of the Catholic Mass arousingly beautiful. *Mea culpa, mea culpa, mea maxima culpa.* The rhythms of the catechism questions' call and response were soothing, calling me home, calling me holy only because I didn't understand them:

> *Do you renounce Satan?*
> *I do renounce him.*
> *And all his works?*
> *I do renounce them.*

I did not know in grade school that I was one of Satan's works because there was no language spoken to describe my desires. *Who made you? God made me.* We didn't talk about our bodies; the naming of parts stopped at the waist. Before I knew the word vagina, before words such as vulva, labia, and clitoris rolled sweet and thick as honey from my tongue and under my tongue, I knew how to create that warm, electric tingling in my groin and belly, knew how to roll the tight button of my clitoris under my thumb to make myself wet, knew how the walls of my vagina felt as they pulsed around my fingers in a muscular hosanna. My body was a temple, a holy mosque of pleasure. Before I knew the word *vagina,* I knew how to make mine happy. Some nights before I fell asleep, I made mine so happy I almost passed out, in flushed and sweaty satisfaction. My vagina, source of temptation. *Halleluiah.*

It is hard to fathom now in a time when nothing is too sacred to reveal—when confession is a popular mode of public expression; when celebrities happily share their diseases, psychological profiles, and need for Viagra; when reality TV sounds less and less scripted—that there was a time when no one talked about anything beyond meatloaf recipes, picking up the dry cleaning, whether it would rain tomorrow, and whose turn it was to do the dishes. We celebrated the Feast of the Immaculate Conception without knowing what conception meant and never thought to ask. I think at some point during third grade we were warned about masturbation, but Sister Anne St. John who gave the lecture was so vague about "touching ourselves in private places" and had so cleverly cloaked the whole lecture within an explanation of hygiene that I made no connection between the act she was describing and what I was doing under my quilt every night.

Last fall in an e-mail exchange with playwright Susan McCully, we made jokes about writing smut. At ten cents a word, we thought we could actually make some money writing. At some point, I complained to Susan that the narrative structure of lesbian erotica—like most narrative structures—followed the rising action of male orgasm: the building to climax, the climax, and then the falling limp. What happens to our own romantic narratives, she asked, where are the near misses and restarts, "the multiplicity and

34

duplicity," the many climaxes, the "glossolalia of women's court-ship and sex"? When I suggested we revise the genre, she laughed. "They pay ten cents a word. How many words do you think you'll get?" I had no words for my desires when I was younger, and now greedily I want them all, I even want to invent my own.

There were eleven people in my family and one bathroom, but with carefully choreographed inhibitions, we somehow man-aged to never see each other naked. Among my mother's many amusing tricks was her ability to get dressed or undressed under her nightgown. The mornings spent watching bras and turtleneck shirts disappear up the long sleeves of her white gown, wondering what secrets were hidden in the voluminous cotton, enjoying the pleasures of this reverse strip tease probably explain my fascination with Dominican nuns, my fantasies about their breasts, areolas sparkly as halos, hidden under white habits, sensuality girdled with the contradiction of black rosary beads, their waists bound tight with the joyful, sorrowful, and glorious mysteries, heavy wooden crosses rubbing their wide hips.

Thanks to the Boston Women's Health Collective and the text *Our Bodies, Ourselves,* which I hid under my mattress, I did not remain wholly ignorant and, when I reached puberty, menstruation was not a horrific surprise. My only ignorance stemmed from my inability to feel anything near physical desire for male genitalia. Boys bored me. But when I thought about it at all, I thought I might just be one of those solitary people who were happiest alone. I had become so adept at masturbating, my fantasies full of Pre-Raphaelite nudes and smiling, red-lipped supermodels that the growing strength of my orgasms was hard to keep hidden. I mean, how many bad dreams could I pretend to have without making my sisters suspicious? Orgasms bubbled through my nervous system like chemical reactants—mimicking the mothballs that danced in soda water or the baking soda and vinegar volcanoes we made in seventh grade science class. I owned all the fireworks of love, and I could do it with one finger.

But a month after I turned fifteen, in the first floor hall of Sacred Heart Academy, just outside of the door to Room 12, on my way to American History class, I finally fell in love with someone other than myself. And I survived the misery of the first few weeks of staring, the giggles, the passing of notes, the worries over does she "like me like me" or just like me, the little gifts of gum, clean gym socks, hair elastics, the furtive touching of fingers and knees that lit up my skin in a pink blushing rush of Fourth of July sparklers, the first time she let me brush her hair, her silken scalp, the first tentative kiss, lips fragile as moth wings. I was in love with Immaculata Aldo, and I found that I liked her vagina, couldn't get enough of it in my mouth, on my fingers, my breasts, my thighs. I loved the smell, I loved the taste. My vagina, her vagina, source of temptation, *praise the Lord of its creation.* All was happiness and bliss and love until mid-summer when I developed a rash between my thighs and an ugly white discharge flowed from my vagina.

I refused to connect this infection with anything we had been doing; however, Immaculata was properly "grossed out" and afraid of catching "it." She began to avoid me and was always busy when I called. Heartbroken, I tried everything to get rid of it—long very hot baths, ice packs held to my labia, changing my underwear three or four times each day, slathering on the few over-the-counter remedies the pharmacy carried. I prayed that, when my period started in a few days, the blood would somehow cleanse my vagina and wash the infection away. It didn't. Nothing worked, the rash burned, my vagina burned, and finally I had to seek the assistance of my mother. *Kiss it, make it better.* She was horrified, claimed she had never had an infection like that, and dragged me to her gynecologist the next afternoon.

There is no more vulnerable position than lying on your back, feet clamped in stirrups, vagina exposed, with only a thin cotton gown protecting your breasts—you remember the material was covered in a pattern of violet sprigs, like the flowers a child would pick for her mother. This is the difficult part of the story; the difficulty is probably why I switched to second person in the first sentence and focused on the pattern in the material of the gown. As a reader, would you rather hear of violets or small bleeding animals caught in traps? Years ago, I spoke with Tim O'Brien at a writers' conference, back before I published anything and was so much braver. At the time, I wanted to know how he could write a battle scene, how he could remember minute details of something so devastating that ended in sparse minutes. None of what he told me will help me here, for this was a battle disguised as healing.

I don't want to confuse this event, my first internal exam, with all my other yearly visits to the gynecologist—even though they are all the same. For a period of five years, I had two appointments a year because of one suspicious pap smear. No matter how kind the physician, he or she is inside you, necessary, but uninvited. The surgeon who removed my uterus held my hand until the anesthesia slowed my breathing. There was no time to say goodbye. *Kiss it, make it better.* After the surgery, morphine kept the pain in check, but it has also made me remember oddly or forget entirely. Sometimes I forget I don't have a uterus.

I do remember how the harsh light glinted off the doctor's metal watchband illuminating a few coarse dark hairs from his wrist. I was so cold, but as one of my punishers, the nurse couldn't offer me a blanket. Speculum, KY Jelly, a long metal spatula, a petri dish—all of these things appeared and then disappeared behind the white cotton sheet draped over my knees. I counted ceiling tiles—seventeen across, fifteen down, what is a six-letter word for a famous Greek lesbian poet? It begins with an "S." I tried to remember the formula for figuring out square footage. I couldn't and so thought I was going crazy. I closed my eyes and prayed to Our Lady of Perpetual Help, chosen because I didn't think there was a particular saint for this occasion. After an eternity of whispering an *Act of Contrition,* I was allowed to sit up and pull the cotton gown over my thighs. I rolled into a ball, knees to chest, arms around my legs. I counted sprigs of violets; I focused on the small tear in the hem of the gown. I negotiated with God. I didn't know then that when you make a bargain with the Catholic God, you always get the raw end of the deal. My face felt wet; my body had been crying while I prayed.

The thin-lipped nurse left the examination room with the red plastic petri dish, and then Dr. Bonner began to question me about my sex life. Not liking my answers, he asked me the same question over and over, six or seven times, louder each time. "Are you fooling around with the boys?" As a raven-haired, red-lipped tease with untamable eyebrows, Immaculata was many things, but she was not by any fabrication a boy. His voice grew louder as I refused to answer, couldn't speak. I was quite sure he could be heard out in the waiting room. This was an inquisition, except unlike the virgin martyrs of early church history, I was guilty. I couldn't breathe when I recognized glints of hell and damnation in Dr. Bonner's eyes. My feet burned, my hands burned, my vagina still burned. Some impulse toward self-preservation kept me from blurting out the truth. I shook my head no so many times my neck began to ache. In those few moments, without being touched, I contacted another insidious, impossible to cure STD called shame. And I began weaving the fiction that became my life to cover my vagina, to smother my body's and heart's desires.

When my mother came into the room, Dr. Bonner assured her that I was still a virgin. I cried with relief. I did not question his diagnosis then, but I've had many discussions with lesbian friends since about when they thought they lost their virginity. Normally, this loss is marked by a penis's penetration of the vagina and the ensuing broken hymen, complete with drops of blood, but what does virginity or the lack of it mean when there is no penis involved? Where do we draw the line? the first finger inside your vagina? the first flick of a tongue on your clit? the first fisting? the first time you straddle a lover's thigh? the first back-aching-arching, you-feel-like-you-might-split-in-half orgasm? Why is it so difficult to write our own narratives?

I was given a prescription for vaginal suppositories, and I assured my worried mother that I could in fact figure out how to insert them myself. They were oval shaped and lavender colored; I bled purple for two weeks, but the infection cleared in less than a week. Immaculata wouldn't return my calls and when school started after Labor Day she wouldn't even look at me—and neither would anyone else. In her need to make a confession and find absolution for loving me, whatever fiction she told our classmates cast me as the village lesbian villain. But, I had made my bargain with God, and I was stuck with it.

I decided to play a different role and begged my parents to let me transfer to public high school, where I knew I could start over, recast my narrative. And I did my best to at least appear straight. I dated boys, I hurt my throat singing soprano in chorus, I claimed to be afraid of bugs and snakes. For fifteen years I lived like everyone else in my neighborhood. I married and had intercourse with my husband by closing my eyes and thinking about anything but other women—the laundry, grocery lists, my job. I hope he thought of other women; otherwise he would have been very bored. We had two daughters, bought an old house, a new car. I went back to college. I smiled all the time, but I was so depressed that all I thought about was dying, all the ways I could die without the act hurting too much. I told my mother I needed help, thought I was going crazy. She thought I just needed to go out to lunch with my girlfriends. How could I tell her I didn't have any girlfriends, that I was afraid to have girlfriends?

This is a lesbian narrative after all, full of digressions, little tensions, and multiple fired flushing climaxes, but still I think I am allowed one princess and one small rescue. My rescue came in the form of my older daughter's third grade teacher, Denise, a tall, thin brunette with eyes as golden brown and full of secrets as a pond. She called and asked me out for coffee because, she said, she was "worried about me." Denise had had a series of disturbing, torturous dreams in which I played a major role. In one, I moved furniture around and around my house. In all of them I had died. "So," she asked, "what's going on?" I clutched her hand, brought it to my mouth, kissed her fingers, held her fist against my cheek until her palm opened and her fingers stroked the side of my face.

For the next few months, my depression loosened its hold. I remembered what it felt like to have a happy vagina, to make another vagina happy. I remembered the way a clit unfurls and swells as it's circled and rubbed by my tongue; I remembered the ocean-full sweet salty taste of joy when a woman comes in my mouth. And I remembered and began the painful rewriting of my life because I had no choice, because I craved another woman's fingers inside my vagina, that muscle-pulsing, effervescent-mothballs-in-soda-water tingle, *hosanna*, my vagina, source of temptation, *praise the Lord, thank you sweet Jesus, grace will lead me home, amen, amen, oh yeah.*

Lord I am not your woman

Susanne Dutton

Lord I am not your woman
at the well
stained and distained, disordered
animal other
I'm easy where I'm put
where appointment awaits postscription
        in a fat dawdled leisure
I lay out my want
        in the shade of the law
I don't say no I
        sleep in it.
How is it then, that as she turns
        from you on pebble-pocked heel
I fever in the splendid craze
of her joy-furied story
How then my fingertips tight
-laced at my collar
        as you wean the world from ash
        in a single drenching slake
and the children
of five husbands press about me
in the wet

It Takes a Village to Rear a Word Weaver

Memoirs of a Black Catholic Girlhood

Mary-Antoinette Smith

"It takes a village to raise a child." This philosophy is an ancient African proverb. . . . Each member of the village would take on the responsibility of the entire group. Children roamed freely from household to household. Adults would parent not only their own children, but all.

—*Veronica Bright*

Growing up black[1] and Roman Catholic during the tempestuous 1960s meant learning to cope compassionately with racism through civil rights nonviolent direct action while adapting to transitional challenges resulting from post-Vatican II changes in the Church. As a young girl, I was aware that momentous occurrences were happening around me, but I was not a primary player in the "action" of either. I was an acutely aware vicarious voyeur of sorts, however, to the impressive and impressionable ways that the adults around me fought for what was right, just, and humane for blacks and

Catholics in America. My parents and my teachers, the Sisters of St. Joseph of Carondelet, were my radical role models who taught me by their actions the importance of "acting out" and/or being unruly in order to fight for and achieve social justice in a myriad of life circumstances. It is to them that I owe a debt of gratitude for my success as a feminist professor, scholar, director of women studies, social justice advocate, and Dominican layperson who loves teaching at a Jesuit institution of higher education.

Serving at Seattle University in these varied vocational capacities for the past twenty years has afforded me opportunities to become more fully integrated in my campus, my spiritual, and my personal lives, while being a role model for my students in the same ways that the adults in my 1960s development as a young grade school girl were for me. All aspects of my career life combine to provide venues for growth that can be both uplifting and challenging at one and the same time, and one of the more recent difficulties I have encountered hit deeply at my core. As a Catholic feminist I was thunderstruck to learn that Pope Benedict XVI, speaking as Cardinal Joseph Ratzinger, had claimed to be "convinced, that what feminism promotes in its radical form is no longer the Christianity that we know; it is another religion." His further declaration that gender theory can lead to the "self-destruction" of the human race because of its alleged blurring of female and male distinctions was equally troubling.[2]

I was disappointed and distressed with the pope's position, and his disorienting pronouncement proved to be a wake-up call/reality check for me. It also opened an unexpected portal through which I began to revisit dormant memories of my parochial school girlhood during the 1960s. Catholic family and parish life was rife with restrictive and confining strictures, and the pope's declaration recalled vivid memories of those oppressive and repressive days of yore. Although challenging at the time, I recognize now that those days were the foundation upon which I began to develop "little activist" tendencies, and the following anecdotal narrative is a reflection on how I came to be the proactive racial and social justice advocate I am today.

The Smiths

My parents met in high school soon after both of their families had migrated from Texas to California. They were high school sweethearts who came from staunch Southern Baptist backgrounds, and it was with deep disappointment that both the maternal and paternal sides of their extended families learned they planned to convert to Roman Catholicism after their civil service marriage. The reason for this conversion was pragmatic and Machiavellian. They wanted their future children to qualify for the benefits of a Catholic education. They had both experienced hardship and deprivation during the Depression, and they were determined that their offspring would never endure the same. They believed wholeheartedly that rearing their children within a solid Catholic family environment, coupled with a solid parochial school education, would ensure their children would not only survive but would guarantee their success. My older and younger brothers and I (the only girl) in the middle were the beneficiaries of this decision.

I am convinced that my parents' radical conversion decision did indeed set the scene for my later successes, but the cost in terms of familial divides between my parents and our maternal and paternal grandparents was high. Their decision created deep hurt at the height of pre–Vatican II rigidities when Catholics were not allowed to attend services at, or even enter into, non-Catholic churches. Consequently, our family was prohibited from attending weddings and funerals for our extended family members, as well as being able to participate in other Baptist church-related functions attended by other family members. It would take years for the pain, rejection, and betrayal to heal. Concurrent with extended family discord, life within The Smith household itself was no idyllic Utopian landscape. We were as dysfunctional as most average American families of the 1960s—replete with an alcoholic father, a codependent mother, an overachieving older son, a quiet, contemplative only daughter, and an underachieving, mischievous younger son.

To add to family discomforts, during the mid-1960s the Smiths were one of the first black families to integrate a block in Inglewood, California, where illegal real estate covenants often prevented blacks from purchasing property in certain neighborhoods. Our suburban home was beautiful, but we struggled throughout the neighborhood with racism and unwelcoming hostilities amidst hopes for the realized goals of the civil rights movement. Within our home there were tensions and hostilities associated with daily traumas, dramas, and familial fragmentations that needed to be managed. Fortunately, these were often offset by our firm grounding in Catholic principles and my parents' proactive and public commitment to civil rights, which provided durable glue that held us tightly bonded together, as did our active parish life at St. John's.

Although I was a quiet, internalized child by nature, observing my parents' hopes for a renewed post–Vatican II Catholic Church, combined with their civil rights activism, inspired in me the desire to cultivate my own "little activisms," which were centered on proving that as a black Catholic female I could be all that I dreamed of being in spite of deliberate and racist obstructions that were set before me by dominant cultural powers that be. I was also richly inspired by the Sisters of St. Joseph who taught at St. John's, who, I noticed, were an intriguing mix of passive supporters of pre–Vatican II doctrines juxtaposed with more radical advocates for the eminent improvements forthcoming with post–Vatican II changes in the Church. While watching my parents and my progressive sister role models, I began with youthful exuberance to meditate frequently on St. Paul's observation in his Letter to the Romans (12:6–8) as a means of self-identifying my innate talents, which I could cultivate as my budding "little activisms" began to emerge: "We have different gifts, according to the grace given us. If a man's gift is prophesying, let him use it in proportion to his faith. If it is serving, let him serve; if it is teaching, let him teach; if it is encouraging, let him encourage; if it is contributing to the needs of others, let him give generously; if it is leadership, let him govern diligently." I gradually discerned that my primary gifts were associated with the articulation and creative use of language.

Soon after this discovery I picked up the habit of storytelling as a means of coping with my family-related challenges, which included financial issues, alcoholic mania, parental arguments in the home, and my worldly difficulties, including minor but hurtful racist occurrences I occasionally encountered outside our home. The habit of oral storytelling became a lifesaving survival mechanism for me in dealing with all of the trauma-drama. Somewhere around second grade I began, in St. John the Evangelist's schoolyard, spinning yarns that rivaled the best of the published literati of the mid-1960s. My stories were fundamentally grounded in *veritas* (i.e., truth, a Dominican motto I would later fully espouse as a layperson), but they exhibited the colorful shadings and flourishes that eventually led me to major in English and to become a writer. At the time, however, simply telling my stories aloud was a useful vehicle for proactively making meaning out of certain chaotic and challenging realities in my home, my school, and my world.

The Schoolyard Kids' Pressure versus the Storyteller

My captive schoolyard listeners marveled daily at my well-crafted narratives, and I reveled in my popularity, which contrasted with the reserve I exhibited within the confines of the alcoholic/codependently dysfunctional Smith household. Before classes, during recesses, at lunchtime, and even after school, I was a storyteller extraordinaire, and my fellow students could not wait to hear the next installments of my broadly drawn tales. The attention was great! As a great tale-teller I was "all that" from second through sixth grade, and it seemed that my popularity would be endless and everlasting. It came as a blunt and hurtful reality, therefore, when my fellow peers and I came back to school after summer vacation to begin seventh grade, and something had changed . . . It seems that prepubescence had morphed into adolescence for many of my peers over summer vacation, and they had returned to school less tolerant of and interested in me and my stories.

As I launched eagerly into my newsy orations about my summer escapades and friendships, someone (or someones) began to reject my stories, and within a week a vicious rumor surfaced and spread that *MarySmith's-a-liar!* This label was a debilitating stigma for me, in addition to having to cope with the overt ostracism that was beginning to manifest across the schoolyard. In addition to being branded *MarySmith's-a-liar!* I was soon silenced. I was no longer permitted to share my "fictions" orally and liberally with my peers. I was abandoned and branded with total and complete finality—*MarySmith's-a-liar!*—period/exclamation point. Alone and misunderstood I was deprived of the sustaining creative activity that had served as my refuge from the horrors of home. I needed desperately to tell my stories as a way of striving and thriving through the crazy-making, in addition to needing the companionship of my listener-peers, but they did not understand my complex and integral need for storytelling as a self-saving coping mechanism. Instead, they branded me into silence with all of the vim, verve, and vigor of their ostracizing camaraderie.

The Sisters of St. Joseph of Carondelet

As I grew through the various phases of my parochial school upbringing at St. John's, I was deeply affected by the Sisters of St. Joseph of Carondelet who were, for the most part, wonderful teachers and guides. That is, until the seventh grade, during which I was convinced that Sr. Loretta Marie was my nemesis. It turned out, however, that she became one of the most important advocates I have ever had in my life. For, unbeknownst to me, she saw great potential in that scrawny little black girl who was always going around "telling stories" to her captive audience of schoolyard peers. She seemed to keep perpetual watch over me, and it always seemed I was constantly in trouble with her for one reason or another. Now that I am an adult, however, I recognize in retrospect that she represented the best of what is meant by the African proverb, "It takes a whole village to raise a child," with which I epigrammatically began this memoir.

Sr. Loretta Marie was my one grade school teacher who took a proactive, concerted interest in my growth and development, and she ultimately guided me toward my potential. As revealed in the following poem, *Parochial Word Weaver*, this radical nun stood up for me unexpectedly and paved the way for my future career as an English professor and writer:

Parochial Word Weaver

"MarySmith's-a-liar-a-liar-a-liar!
MarySmith's-a-liar-a-liar-She-lies!

MarySmith's-a-liar-a-liar-a-liar! MarySmith's-a-liar-a-liar-She-lies!"
"MarySmith's-a-liar-a-liar-a-liar!
MarySmith's-a-liar-a-liar-She-lies!
MarySmith's-a-liar-a-liar-a-liar! MarySmith's-a-liar-a-liar-She-lies!"

Over and over they stammered and taunted
    chanting away, *"MarySmith-She-lies!"*
Schoolyard kids collectively yelling
    the run-on claim of my weaving of tales
Lies they were—admittedly, grand and tall

Laden with imagery, with character and plot
He saids, and she saids, and they dids, and more . . .
What drove me to tell "whoppers" I never quite knew
But it certainly was something I was compelled by nature to do
On and on, imagination abounding
I orally spun my broadly drawn tales
But soon the schoolyard kids grew weary of hearing
And that's when they branded me that compound name
MarySmith's-a-liar-a-liar-She-lies!
A debilitating stigma; an internal stigmata
    the bleeding of sores, inward and deep
Wounded—Belittled—Silenced—Abhorred
Yet oozing to speak and orate some more
Recesses were lonely.
Lunch times alone.
Or Mass with the Sisters in the Chapel at noon.
Visibly silent but still word weaving
    imaginary tales in my head and my heart
Then came the day of forgiveness, reprieve
    from an unlikely source—Sister Loretta Marie
Who calmly invoked our homeroom class to *"Silence!!!!*
Attention!!!!"
She said she had something important to say . . .
For she'd heard troubling rumors of the ostracization
    of one of their pre-pubescent peers
"A clever young girl—one that's gifted and talented . . .
Naive little children, you have misunderstood
MarySmith's not *a-liar*—not *a-liar* at all.
She's a weaver of words unlike any other . . .
    a teller of tales in a pedestrian way;
But mark *my words,* little judgmental ears,
    her skills will grow into meaningful writing someday."
Exonerated—Acquitted—again one of the Fold
    my liberated voice was launched that day
Freed of the stigma; the stigmata dried up
No-more-MarySmith's-a-liar-a-liar-a-liar!
MarySmith's-a-liar-a-liar-No-more!

She's newly renamed, more appropriately now: *Mistress-Spinner-of-Stories-the-Weaver-of-Tales!*

From the day Sr. Loretta Marie made this protective pronouncement I was fully and freely received back amongst my peers. It was as simple as that. She proclaimed my innocence, and I was once again embraced by the fold. What presence, what power, what protective insight and *curas personalis,* care of the person, as only one who understands the importance of it taking a village to raise a child. But my memoir does not end here, for as all good Catholic school girls did at the time, and in spite of Sr. Loretta Marie's valiant voicing of my virtuous storytelling intentions, I was compelled to make my weekly trip to the confessional to tell Father McCaffrey what had happened: "Oh bless me, Father, for I have sinned. It has been a week since my last confession. These are my sins . . . Father, Father, the school kids in my class have been saying I'm a liar, liar, liar, because I tell stories *aaalllll* the time, but for some reason this week Sr. Loretta Marie told the *whoooole* class that I'm not a liar at all. She said I'm a really talented storyteller who will probably grow up to be a writer someday. Oh Father, oh Father, have I *reeeeaaally* been lying!!!? or not? I mean I know that my stories really aren't true, but I tell them all the same . . ."

Trying very hard to repress a chuckle, Father treated my inquiring sinful exuberance with due diligence and carefully explained that while it was, of course, a sin to tell lies, he agreed with Sister Loretta Marie's explanation of my storytelling prowess and expertise. To ensure that I understood the gravity of telling lies, as opposed to creating fictions, however, he wanted to make sure I was utterly clear on the distinction between the two. He saw fitting, therefore, to give me an appropriate penance: "My child, you're to say three whole rosaries everyday for the next week, and then I look forward to hearing your *honest* confession next Friday. Go with God, my child." My grateful reply was, "Oh, thank you, thank you, Father . . ." as I fully understood the import of the penance as a means of making restitution for those fictions that perhaps were indeed lies, rather than mere narrative falsehoods.

Yet again, I am reminded of the "It takes a whole village to raise a child" adage, for this truly is what Sister Loretta Marie and Father McCaffrey were doing in partnership to shape and guide me appropriately as a good Catholic girl, while concurrently fostering what they clearly perceived as a natural giftedness for storytelling.

Concluding Word Weaver Wisdom

Writing this memoir has helped me realize my great appreciation for Sr. Loretta Marie's rare and radical advocacy of me—a perpetual parochial prevaricator with budding talent. She was a sage seer, a perceptive educator, and a humane leader, and given my success as a scholarly and creative writer, she was obviously accurate in her prophetic assessment of me. However unbeknownst to me at the time, she conscientiously served as a path builder and visionary protectress of what would later evolve into an extraordinary career for me, and her *curas personalis* has inspired in me the same approach: as a feminist educator and social justice advocate who takes a perceptive stance as a "village leader" in guiding my students toward becoming whole persons dedicated to a life of service and committed to achieving a just and humane world.

Something else happened that day, as well, and it has taken me years to recognize the bittersweetness of what was gained and what was lost as a consequence. Even though I was completely exonerated from being *MarySmith-the-Liar* from that day forth, I stopped telling stories orally as a result of that experience. Oral traditions are a natural part of my African cultural heritage, but I lost my courage for oral storytelling from that point on. My one reprieve comes, however, from the fact that I transitioned from orality to writing, for there was nothing short of death itself that could keep me from expressing myself through words. It is just that, now, the written word serves as my primary and preferred safe-space genre as an academic, spiritual, and creative writer. And while I never lie in my writing, I have been known to "turn a phrase" to convenient advantage from time to time, as a gifted and successful WordSmith and Word Weaver extraordinaire should occasionally manage to do.

Notes

1. During the 1960s the terms *black* and *negro* were commonly used to identify the ethnicity of those of us who now refer to ourselves as African Americans. Throughout this memoir these terms are used interchangeably, but mainly with reference to the time periods during which the narrative chronologically takes place.

2. Letter to the Bishops of the Catholic Church on the Collaboration of Men and Women in the Church and the World.

Facts of the world I

Lauren K. Alleyne

On the screen, the pilgrims
clutched their candles
and rosaries, their fingers
worrying the beads in unison
as experts weighed in—the wary
the believers, the downright
skeptical. Although
my mother's prized silver chaplet
hung in the prayer room
under a statue of Mary,
Mom tells us she didn't believe
the hype about the Virgin
for years, until one night
she dreamt herself
standing beyond the world—
not in space, exactly,
just beyond—watching.
How the earth's spinning grew
faster, careening, unsteady
and it seemed both her heart and the blur
would explode with whirling.
How the beads appeared

in her hands and she prayed
decade after decade
and like a terrified child
who finds itself held
the earth hiccoughed, calmed.
After that, Mom says, *I believed.*

We turn back to the screen,
to the pilgrims, transfixed,
their arms outstretched
their eyes trained
on something beyond
the camera's reach.
Some sobbed hysteric
prayers, the voiceover
translating their fervor
with discordant steadiness—
people are reporting miracles:
healings, rosaries turning to gold,
visions of the sun pulsating in the sky . . .
The broadcast ends
with a picture of the globe
suspended in the stratosphere,
two hands poised below
as if to catch the giant ball.
Mom turns off the television
and we move on
to homework and Sunday chores:
The hours spin past.
We do not know when
it happens,
but there, in the prayer room,
above the chapel, beneath the glow-
in-the-dark statue of Our Lady,
my mother's rosary gleams,
inexplicably, gold . . .

girltruth

Stasha Ginsburg

Women always walk in two worlds. Born into the "Adam's world" of culture consistently "named" from male life-experiences, we find ourselves with language and categories that do not fit or name our experience as girl children or female adolescents. We early come to know "girltruth," which is experience without a language.[1]

I didn't know what it was called until recently, or that it was something I might temporarily disconnect from. Mine was spunky and full of voice. It got me into trouble in Catholic school on numerous occasions. The first time was a declaration at age nine that there is no such thing as heaven and hell. I said, quite matter of fact, "Heaven is what you make it and so it is different for you than it is for me." The Catholic school teachers looked at me as if I had just committed an enormous sin. I also got into trouble for crossing each of the angels off my sheet. We were supposed to "be good" each week of Lent. If we sinned, we were to cross out an angel. They sent me to the principal's office and I declared, "But you gave me original sin! How am I supposed to keep my angels if I'm bad because I was born?" I don't recall what they had to say.

Girltruth gave me full-belly permission to be equal to boys. It made sure I knew I was smart, athletic, and talented. It encouraged me to compete with boys in contests, races, and spelling bees. In my fatherless family, my Italian grandfather treated boys differently than girls, in a way that felt like a secret handshake to a club I wasn't invited to attend. In Catholic school, boys seemed to have a privilege that I wasn't allowed to participate in. Girltruth was my first revolutionary ally.

I decided to create my own clubs with secret languages and handshakes. I challenged the boys to races and kiss-or-kill games. I ran for class president and won at age nine because girls have a right to be president. I was the only girl on the boys' Little League Team. I could make as good a fort as any. I jumped out of trees in winter. I went alone into dark places retrieving treasures.

My girltruth declared freedom to my mother and nonna, assuming that they knew nothing of it at all. Their black-and-white womantruth was explosive but often defensive and rigid. They often referred to church, God, or politics in a way that made authority seem dangerous, punishing, and judging. No matter. For a brief time, girltruth was a wild warrior child questioning every rule, boundary, and limiting statement such as "Children should be seen and not heard," "Only boys can be altar boys," "Kissing will give you babies."

My girltruth believed in magic and imagination. She knew you could learn a lot from trees and that you could know things ahead of time without knowing how you knew. She knew that just one person in the magical space with a cranky attitude was enough to kill the magic for everyone. She knew that the church didn't feel magical, but nature did.

When I reached puberty and it was time to be confirmed a young adult by the St. Sebastian Catholic Church, I tried naming myself after my favorite saint, Saint Francis Xavier of Assisi. I wanted to shorten it to Xavier because I thought it would be cool to have a new name that began with the X on a pirate's treasure map. I also wanted to be as important in the eyes of the church, to God, as boys. Why is God a man? Why did a woman grow out of a guy's ribs? Why did woman tempt man? And why do I have original sin now because of it? My opinions and questions embarrassed the priest. "We just don't do it that way. You cannot have a boy's name, that is not acceptable." I pleaded but had to settle on the name Monica. The wind in my sails died and my fire got blown out. Although I didn't realize it, I felt a dangerous poison take seed in me. I was now confirmed in the eyes of God, a girl becoming a woman, a possible temptress, a sinner, maybe pure and untouchable if I strived to be like Mary, but forever shamed with original sin, descendent of women, who are original sin makers.

My girltruth closed itself tightly inside of me around puberty and slept for a long, long time. Was she scared? Had she given up? Was she a victim? Or like Persephone descending or Sleeping Beauty lost in a hundred-year sleep—was this an essential part of the transformative story of her becoming, separate from what church or some other authority deemed an appropriate rite of passage?

Without her I felt a victim to the status-quo world around me, split temporarily from the effortless knowing and spunk that had been my compass. I felt tricked into relying on authority while rebelling self-destructively in secret. I had to learn to navigate a world with rules that often didn't make sense.

Occasionally girltruth opened herself like the eyes of a sphinx, in between the spaces surrounding the oppression of a perfectly valid and beautiful coming of age, voice, identity, and wild woman-ness. She would witness me, eye me up and down, and ask, before closing her eyes, "Who are you? What do you know, girl, what do you know?"

Girltruth and I grew into each other in the wild and primitive forest and nature playgrounds in upper Michigan when I was eight. My girltruth sprouted like from a trillium seed, took root and grew delicate and wild in the forest among pine trees, oak, birch, fern, and moss. She has been plucked and overlooked. Sometimes she wilts, and sometimes she is preserved. She waits quietly in the dead of winter. Every spring, when she returns, she wants us to know: she is an important endangered species.

I want to protect and honor the vulnerable strength of girl-truth. Girltruth and trilliums have taught me the true meaning of a trinity. Because of this I have more courage to walk in the world as I know it—a gentle warrior father holding the fiercely compassionate and revolutionary hand of my inner mother, so that my inner child or girltruth can continue to blossom her living experiences into wisdom.

Note

1. Elizabeth Dodson Gray, foreword, *Walking in Two Worlds*.

the Easter fear

Susanne Dutton

For my own sake I came early
to flood the still warm vacancies of your death
with sweet oils
finding
here this man bent
over the earth
who gives way to you
lets you take over.
his shoulder falls away
into yours as he hacks at the ground
his profile, brow to lip, runs
like watery dye into yours
and he takes on your colors
brown purple
loses even the sun-rough backs
of his hands to you,
goes away so well for you
becomes a yes—
doing you,
except for some small resistance
insistence on himself
as he moves closer, a no—

not doing you.
so I am walking away:
the hope-stricken,
fear-quickened
pointy-shaped steps of religion, oil jostling
to an ooze in my fingers, a pungent spatter
in my skirts,
to a safe place
at a distance—
out of range of his little claims against you
where I turn to look back,
where he gives himself up
absolutely, gardener amidst the tombs no longer
but leans down,
reaching out
his hand to trace circles in the sand
as men lose grip
of stones.

Part Two

The Sorrowful Mysteries

Holy Thursday: The Passion

Lauren K. Alleyne

I have lost my passion. Why should I keep it
since what is kept must be adulterated?

—*T.S. Eliot, Gerontion*

Today, the keenness of red makes her weep;
to smile takes strength to move any mountain.
It begins: *On the night He was betrayed . . .*
she knows the story: Eat. Drink. Remember.
Always the body. Broken. Like failed fast.
Between devout and deserter a kiss,
coin, a taste for—, bittersweet surrender
And two thousand years. Too late to anoint
His feet with oil or tears, to baptize them
With sorrow and her worthless hands. She knows
shame: the cock's three-time crow mocking her heart;
its yearning despite. Her faith, an old shoe,
a false note, a key
               —It will not fit true.

That Easter

Leonore Wilson

I remember how cold it was that Easter, a bitter cold that kept us in as if it were winter, but the sun was out, the sun was a big deception in the sky. We were all at dinner—picture the ham, mashed potatoes, dyed eggs, the jelly beans. Then the phone rang. My mother answered. The dispatcher said people saw a naked woman running through traffic, she was running like a scared doe in headlights. They couldn't shout her down or weave her in. They asked us if we had seen her, that she was last spotted running into the open field in back of the house. The police wanted to know if they could come up to the ranch and find her. A naked girl? Or was it a woman? My mother said it didn't matter, no we hadn't seen her. Then my husband left the table as if he were a doctor and this was his call. He ran out of the house and so did our boys. I was left with my mother at the table. We were the women. The food like a big accident before us. We ate the ham, the salad, drank our milk in silence to the sirens.

My husband came back. He said something about her wearing only underwear, big panties, nothing fancy, and that she had lived in the field for three days. He said she was nothing to look at really. In fact she looked like a dog, dog-ugly. He asked if I would give her a sweatshirt, some pants. I went to the laundry room, picked out the pink ones I hated, the color of peonies.

Later I saw her at a distance. They had her handcuffed. They were taking her down the mountain. It was starting to rain. She had her head down, the way Jesus had his head hung, ready for the crucifixion; she was that scrawny. I put my body in her body. She was wearing my clothes. My husband told me she kept telling the cops that she was a mother, that no mother should be treated with handcuffs, that she was no danger. The cop said she was covered with bruises, that her husband had beaten her and left her on the highway, that she wanted to die in the field where she first met him, her lover. The cop said she was on drugs and loony. He said she'd probably go back to her husband. That they always do. These strays, these losers.

That was ten years ago, but I still think of her. This woman, not the only inconsolable stray I've found on my rural road, in this paradise called Napa, this manna of land fluted by canyons, sharpened by cliffs. Wappo territory where wild irises bloom their white flags from the portholes of meadows. There've been others. Other women. The woman with purple welts around her neck, scourged neck of the black and blue, weeping near her stalled U-Haul and the oversized drunken tattoo of a man. Or the woman whose husband drove his black sedan behind her as she walked the dotted line, the mean bumper of his souped-up car butting up against her like a bull. But it was she, the woman discovered on Easter, who remains in my center like the blue throat of the owl in the center of moonlight. She the vixen's red breath coming out of the garden and into the pitch. She emerging from the earth-bed like Persephone released from Hades, but returning to Hades. She, the matted camellia, the numbed apostrophe of the killdeer stirred from the cinders. Who is she, whose handiwork? Whose heat did she trigger? What ownership? Who was she, that threadbare girl of skin and ribs, feeling invisible, that field witch? Did anyone ask her; what are you feeling, do you feel anything, as they cuffed her bare feet, stuffed her in back of that cop car? Was she bound and flogged before he, her lover, her spouse, tossed her out like rotten trash? Is there any way to explain her naked body? Her naked fingers? Her fallen legs collapsing under her like unplayed cards?

I think of her, of all the women I have found in my country, their shadows writhe within me. I who have stayed silent. They with their loosened hair, stained with soil and blood, drugged eyes glazed forever on the black chart of amnesia. There have been many in these hills, this valley. Wild, hard women. Endangered sisters. Their heaped colors suddenly gone ashen like the cloudiness that forms over winter blacktop. They who scratch themselves, who urinate, who stay in unspeakable loneliness, their feminine power routed backward like miles of barbwire. They are homeless cursed women, naughty women, the words stolen out of their teeth like bread. They who would rather choke than be vulgar.

How can I wrap my house in sleep thinking of them, thinking of her making a fire of wet wood, telling stories to herself, singing lullabies, nursing the tragedy of her sex. I pace the floor thinking of her. I poke my spade into the dry loam and think of her. I find her everywhere. I have learned her by heart. I have worn her close to my body. For she is my body. She is the foundling of the woods, the one slip of tongue, the liquid mist that burns off the highway as the new day forms.

I want to know who touched the match to her flesh, who left her blanketless in the frost as I stoked and blazed my stove. I know she was there in the twilight and thorns. I've felt her mouth on mine like a lump of bitter jelly all those times alcohol was fire on my breath. The times I starved myself with pills in my pocket, wanting love, wanting the brisk taste of airports and ferries, I've been her. The times I wanted the impermissible, I've been her. Discontent as a cormorant that pokes around the corpses of roses, wanting to be fractured, exiled under the floss of many petals, I've been her. Wanting to be seduced by that floral nard. Me, in the snowstorm of unimaginable longing while the hangman's noose rose inside my chest, taunting, taunting. I too tried on death too many times. I who wore my own bruises like badges around my jaw. I of steely posture.

Why?

I lowered myself in the chaparral, afraid, my breasts full of milk, my hair disheveled. I thought I could stand betrayal, that I could spill myself like purple vetch, like legend down the lush gametrails into drink. What soothed me? Sometimes mint in the mouth, sometimes the pearl-gray mist. I wanted to be like my ancestors. I wanted to be strong as shattered rock, as basalt mortars. I didn't think it right that a woman go off like a kettle full boil. But I was proud and half-blind. I was a stuttering tadpole. A spectacle. An odd empty thing.

I was a master of nothing. I wrestled with the serpent inside me, the female totem of melancholy. Me with my teacups and miniature cakes. I sucked in my midnights, my howls and my whelps. Why? How many dead girls like me smelled of old lunatic lies?

My sentence was mine: my well-piped breeding, my pilgrim dreams. Guardian of chandeliers, when my heart was always squawking like an interior swan.

Be damned the well-scrubbed house, the family snapshots. Be damned the flowers of Hell, the ostracized penance, the lowermost regions, Lethe's spell where Eurydice wastes away with Persephone. Be damned if the dark snake of Eden flew out of my mouth. I want the Easter woman at my table, I want her story. I want to take her groggy hand, lead her away from the fettered ring, the life of sacrifice, of thick-scented curses. My tongue dips into the chewed meat of thistled honey when I say this. Mothering is the dilation of feathers. Forget the flower-pressed face concealing its failures, bleeding its kindness like a parasite. Inside our smile is the knife-grind, the winged lion. What abscesses in our flesh—not our humiliation, nor our quarrel, but our rising.

Our Lady of the Library

Sarah Colona

for WF

1.

Violets wither at her fingertips.

2.

In sleep, an infestation. Walls quiver.
A writhing mass crawls head downward.
On each pinched face: eyes still shut.
Pink nostrils flared.

3.

Crow-flowers, Meadowsweet, Nettles:
Here too, a language you must learn.

4.

A winged-serpent in *my* garden?
Surely, you've the wrong house.

5.

Oh! Our Lady of the Library,
Of the dust-caked, hushed womb.

6.

Light a candle. Name it God's mistake.
Light another. Call it Shock.

7.

Pocket the dollars left below Mary's frown.

8.

I carry Grief—my hands *just so*.

9.

I write Cadmus:
Teeth in a field.
Stones and what follows.
Look the damn thing up!

10.

See how I am sewn up with secrets.
Stone-bellied. Wolf perpetually abed.

For the Vatican Dress Code

Annarose Fitzgerald

Yes, I forgive him, the round little man
In his bright green shirt and black suspenders
Long pants in Rome mid-June
For hissing at me and tapping his shoulders when I turned
    around
Like he wanted to start a children's game
For furrowing his fat brows at me in contempt
For boring his eyes into my bare back
As I was already burning with shame
Doing my best as I walked past Saint Barbara with her left
    breast exposed
All because of a purple halter top
Purple, the color of princes and Advent

Yes, I forgive him, because in all his roundness
How could he have known what it was like
For someone with steep curves and angles
Who had all too recently survived being shrouded in plaid
Told that her curves and angles were beautiful
So long as her prom date had never seen or touched them
Told that her shapes were hers to give
But God's to decide when and how

And how could he, in all his roundness, have known what it was like
To have her shapes snatched once again
To lie to herself that this tradition is dead and powerless
To make her scream?

Nothing Soup

Dedicated to Helusia Biadaszkiewicz

K. Biadaszkiewicz

Somewhere between St. Mary's and St. Inigoes, there is a narrow, unpaved road that leads to a small cottage, its front yard bursting with the crimsons and blues and yellows of carefully tended flowers. Not far from the cottage is the river, and early in the morning, the old woman who lives in the cottage walks to the river to watch the ripples catch the early sunlight. It is something she has done for a very long time without fail, as the devout begin each day with prayer.

Katrina was in Sister Mary Bernice's third grade when Synek came. Babies were born at home in those days, and for Katrina and her family, home was half a rented rowhouse with a small plot of hollyhocks, poppies, and bachelor buttons in the front yard, on the down side of Fells Point. None of the five little girls was allowed upstairs, and Kazia, the oldest, took Musia's place as best she could, so when Tatusz brought down their pillows and bed linens, Kazia set them up on the floor in front of the stove and told her sisters they would pretend that they were all brave soldiers fighting the Kaiser.

For two days, after a breakfast of stale cookies and sweet vanilla water, the little soldiers marched to school with carefully

71

but unevenly braided hair and somewhat rumpled uniforms, carrying lunch baskets filled only with apples from the barrel under the stairs and a quantity of chipped saltines. For two nights, lying on the hard floor, they tried to concentrate on Kazia's lullabies, especially when her voice would give out and they could plainly hear their mother's weak cries from the bedroom above them.

On the third morning Tatusz came slowly downstairs, his face drawn and pale, his large, deep eyes puffed and red. He gathered his daughters around him and hugged each one of them. He cleared his throat. "You had a little brother," he said. "He was . . . He was called Synek . . ."

"Can we go upstairs and see him now?" asked Janja.

"No, you can't."

"Why?"

"Because he's not upstairs."

"Then where is he?"

"In heaven," said Tatusz.

"Can we see Musia, then?"

"Is she in heaven, too?"

"No," he said. "But she is very, very weak. She needs to rest, and we need to help her. When you get home from school, if she is feeling well enough, you may see her."

That day at school, Katrina could not keep her mind on her work. She asked the Blessed Virgin on her necklace to help her concentrate, but it didn't work. Sister Mary Bernice rapped her knuckles with a yardstick for fooling with the necklace and made her stay after school to finish her arithmetic—the subject she hated the most. What was the use of counting *how many* or *how much*, if people were crying, or homesick, or afraid?

Sitting alone in the quiet classroom, all she could hear was the clock ticking. All she could think of was running home and hurrying up the stairs to hug her mother. Surely if she tried hard enough she could find a way to help Musia get well again. The tall, black-robed figure peeked in the hallway door and Katrina quickly lowered her head and pretended to be adding a column of numbers. Yardstick in hand, the figure in black robes and thick-heeled black shoes walked back to the little girl's desk and stood over her.

Katrina's mind went blank. Numbers, and what they were and what they weren't and what they might be and what they could never be, blurred and dissolved before her eyes.

More tears rolled down her face and plopped on the paper where tidy rows of correct answers ought to have been written. The little girl braced herself for another strike of the yardstick.

"Why are you crying?" demanded the nun.

"My mother had a baby."

"A child is a blessing from the Lord."

"Yes, Sister Mary Bernice."

"Instead of sitting here whimpering you should have finished your work so you could help your mother with the baby."

"I can't."

"Shame on you."

"But he's in heaven."

"You may finish your work tomorrow," said Sister Mary Bernice, lifting the wet arithmetic paper carefully off the desk, so as not to tear it. "But before you leave you must pray for God's forgiveness. Seven Hail Marys."

"Yes, Sister Mary Bernice."

"Take your time, young lady. The Holy Mother does not like you to rush."

"Yes, Sister Mary—"

"Enough, enough. I'll be out in the hall."

"Yes, Sister—"

Katrina immediately bowed her head and began to pray. In no time at all she had completed five of the Hail Marys. She stole a look around the room. She was alone again. She took a deep breath. Two more, and she could go home. Two more, and she would have helped Musia get well. Two more and she would have been forgiven. Two more and maybe she would know what it was that she had to be forgiven for. Then she saw it.

The shiny dime was on the desk in front of her, Emily's desk. Emily, whose parents owned a huge brick home and whose hair was as fine as angel's hair. Emily, whose winter coat and hat were fur lined, and who brought sliced roast beef or chicken salad or sliced baked ham sandwiches with purple grapes and chocolate cakes for lunch. Emily, whose parents always sat in the front pew at high mass. Emily, whose purse was always bulging with coins. Surely she had forgotten about this one. Or, more likely, the Virgin Mother herself knew how much Musia needed her strength back. The Holy Mother had heard Katrina's first five Hail Marys and had placed the coin there for her to find. Katrina got up out of her seat, took a quick look around the room, and slipped the coin into her pocket. Then Katrina closed her eyes and said seven additional Hail Marys, to show her gratitude.

Katrina hurried down the hall and out the door. She skipped down the sidewalk and ran all the way to the bakery, where she ordered a large loaf of fresh bread. She waited while Mrs. Mullins wrapped the bread in crisp white paper.

Katrina gave Mrs. Mullins the dime. All the way home she imagined how happy Musia and Tatusz would be. Surely this was what the Holy Mother had intended. Surely this would be the bread that would help Musia to have strength enough to come downstairs again, the way she used to.

Katrina ran most of the way home. She was worried that her family might wonder where she was. But when she arrived home nobody seemed to notice that she was late. Doctor Mihalik was there, standing at the foot of the stairway talking quietly to Tatusz. They shook hands and the doctor left. When Tatusz led Katrina upstairs, she carried the white parcel under her arm, carefully so as not to squish it.

Katrina walked into the bedroom. The air was stuffy.

"It's Katrina to see you," whispered Tatusz.

The woman on the bed opened her eyes very slightly. Katrina's throat began to hurt. She had never seen her mother look so tired. The little girl leaned on the bed to kiss her mother. The woman groaned.

"You must not touch the bed!" whispered Tatusz. Musia's lips moved, but Katrina could not hear the words. Katrina bent over and carefully kissed her mother's hand. It was cold. Katrina swallowed hard and forced herself to smile.

"I've brought you a surprise," she said. "Look, Musia. It's for you." Katrina's heart filled. She imagined how her mother would bite into the soft bread and smile. Soon she would sit up and put her arms around Katrina again and hug her. Katrina gently placed the crisp white parcel on the bed at her mother's side. Surely at any moment her mother would smell the wonderful aroma and open the package. But the woman in the bed did not move.

"Katrina has brought something for you," whispered Tatusz gently. He leaned over and Musia spoke into his ear. Her lips moved slowly, as if in a dream. "Musia cannot open the package, Katrina. Please do it for her."

Katrina opened the package and held it out for her mother. The woman in the bed slowly opened her eyes. When she saw the bread she began to cry. Again Tatusz leaned over and his wife spoke into his ear. He stood up and asked Katrina where the bread had come from.

"I bought it."

"Where did you get the money?" Katrina told how she had found the dime on Emily's desk. "You must go to the priest and tell him what you have done, and then you must go and tell Emily, too," said Tatusz. "And you must give her this." He reached into his pocket and took out a thin, well-worn coin purse. He took a dime out of the coin purse and placed it in Katrina's hand.

Emily just smiled and stuffed the dime into her crowded purse. The priest, on the other hand, wanted more information. Katrina confessed to having taken the dime so that her mother would get her strength back. The priest told Katrina what prayers to say, and how many, and that she should say them at mass on Sunday when she went with her parents and sisters.

"I don't know if Musia will be able to go to mass this Sunday," Katrina said, her throat beginning to hurt again.

"Then you must help her so she can attend," said the priest.

"I try to help," began Katrina. "But she had a little baby and he died. She can't even sit up."

"Don't you know that if your mother doesn't come to mass on Sunday, she will burn in hell for all eternity?"

"Yes, Father."

"Good girl. Now go in peace."

A horrible weight pushed down on Katrina as she stumbled out of the church and onto the sidewalk. Her throat hurt so much that she had trouble breathing. Her feet became heavy and would not cooperate; they had forgotten how to carry her from one place to another by taking turns, one in front of the other.

And so it happened that she ended up far from home, way down by the harbor, watching the sunlight play against the ripples in the water. She tried to stop thinking of what the priest had said, but the rhythm of his voice kept pounding in her ears.

Finally, unable to bear the din any longer, Katrina slipped the Blessed Virgin necklace from her throat, tossed it into the water, and watched it disappear.

There was a kind of breeze, dancing above the water, causing ripples to glisten, then skipping toward her, bringing a mist, and within it, a tiny wisp of something as invigorating as fresh air and as sweet as a dream she didn't want to wake up from.

And from that mist, the little girl conjured her very own Blessed Virgin, a new and improved version, one who understood everything she thought about and wondered about and hoped for, and all the mysterious feelings that swirled around inside.

This was to be the same Blessed Virgin who would carry Katrina safely through the fire and the Great Depression, and the War, and the birth of her own children. She was the one who would guide Katrina through the darkness and terror and joys of her own memories, and would ask nothing of her in return. No requisite confessions, no forced prayers, and no yardstick knuckles.

The new Blessed Virgin even sensed how Katrina hated arithmetic, so she never demanded to know how many or how much of anything, and was perfectly happy when Katrina filled everything to the very top. The new Holy Mother never required spoken prayers, but understood without being told what was in Katrina's heart. And as it turned out, Katrina's heart was often full of what many would call prayer. Best of all, She gave Katrina strange powers to see beauty where others saw nothing, and to bring song to places where others heard nothing. In this way Katrina was able to surprise even the warblers who nibbled on stale cookie crumbs on that long-ago day when the little girl returned home, singing a little song nobody had ever heard.

She did help Musia to get well, and was a source of strength for both her parents, although they never fully recovered from the loss of their baby boy. When there was money, Musia would send Katrina or Janja to the butcher's for sausages and to the tavern for pails of beer. When there was no money, Musia would make "nothing soup" from eggs and milk and a little sugar. In their last photograph Musia and Tatusz looked like two people old long before their time, a fat old woman and a skinny old man, oceans away from the young bride and groom photographed in Krakow, when their eyes had shone with hope.

Katrina, too, is a fat old woman, now in her eighty-fifth year. But her face is bright, and the sparkle in her eyes sometimes resembles that of a young third grader, full of wonder and delight.

Her garden is a showplace in the low country between St. Inigoes and St. Mary's, far from Fells Point and its churches.

Late on Sunday mornings she welcomes friends with fresh brewed coffee and slices of warm Polish coffee cake. Early most every other morning she hurries outdoors to praise the air and the wind and the first rays of sunshine, no matter the weather.

She shovels her own walk, mows her own lawn, and takes special pride in her flower garden, watering and weeding and gathering bouquets of coreopsis and hollyhocks and poppies and bachelor buttons, while singing a little song nobody has ever heard.

Nailing My Backbone to the Cross

Donna J. Gelagotis Lee

—Athens, Greece, c. 1987

The priest watches the coin box. Holy
Saturday. Even the faithless come.
Even the dubious will light a candle

and then a firecracker and throw it
at the feet of the believers.
The priest motions for me to move

away if I am not putting coins
in the box, as if each light
were a passage to heaven. Pay for it.

I too am a believer. I pray. I hold
onto palms and fan myself. I suck up
to the religion of the masses. I forgive

all those with hammers, as I cut
my wood after I measure, and nail
my faith to the cross.

True Confessions

Patti See

The summer Coke changed its recipe back
to Classic and Sally Jesse Raphael moved from radio
to TV, I sweltered over a grill in the screened Falls
Drive-In kitchen turning burgers and dropping fries;
or I fitted trays to car windows, waiting for fifteen
to bump into sixteen and transform me from carhop

to sultry teen beauty. The Farrrah-haired carhops,
busty and tan, swiveled aprons and necks. Down my back
hung a kinky mop I'd hid behind for all of my fifteen
years. Most shifts I watched the highway, radios
blasting from cars driving past; or I memorized a fried
food litany: pizza burger, pronto pup, ribette—all falling

into a chain—zebra cone, slop, polar bear. Chippewa Falls
girls were separated, hot items from cold. An older carhop
told me dropping cheese curds into the deep fryer,
You Catholic girls have it easy, no guilt, just pay-back
with Novenas. I shrugged, listening for some distant radio.
A week later we guzzled Andre pink bought for $2.15

a bottle and closed Babe's Bar where even fifteen
was old enough. After my first acknowledged fall
it got easier to feign experience, turn up the radio
with public school boys and their dollar tips. I carhopped
the weeks away to Fridays, when I ran to the bank and back,
or face to face confessed my sins, still afraid of frying

in hell. The worst I penanced alone, silently deep frying
away with half-chicken Sunday dinners. At fifteen
a Hail Mary for every boy or Glory Be for every beer backed
up my lies quick as a reorder slip. I spent slow days at the Falls
playing tic-tac-toe alone and learned from the other carhops
that most boys were really not the heroes that made radio

love songs, but a trick of x's and oh's. I tuned the radio
with one hand, slid patties into buns or bagged fries
with the other, and became the only known carhop
who delivered a six-pak of cones in one trip. At fifteen
I carved my name into the red counter of the Falls
Drive-In, joining thirty years of names etched back

on June days playing the same greasy radio, girls
a breath past fifteen, frying in the same tiny kitchen,
knowing a boy has fallen when he sticks to you
like a tray to a window. And wondering
if—like carhops—only the start of an engine
or the honk of a horn can bring him back.

Resolution

Lauren K. Alleyne

If offered in all its sweetness, the world,
she will not turn. To atone the body,
its complicated want; she must be *good*.
And it will begin here—she was ready.

The plan: to wake every morning at dawn,
reflect, read her bible, pray the rosary.
She will make a habit of devotion,
drape her flesh in new faith, wear it wholly.

Her morning meal will be humble, only
water will cross her lips until evening
—for these forty days she will be empty,
this daughter of Eve—hunger redeeming
her sins of inheritance, commission;
her wayward heart, its caution of Eden.

Excuse me for this, Sister Mary:

Ava C. Cipri

I believe in reincarnation, the eternal
exchange of one worn
thread-bare garment
for another. I've known the haunting
tick of time's salty debris on my tile
floor after shaking my clothes out,
wondering whose misplaced day I found.
This is how I learned:
I died in old age, slow
and lonely once as a sea
merchant's wife, loosening the gum
of oysters with a paring knife,
counting my husband closer
with each mollusk I severed.
I've watched the farthest wake come
in from the horizon and thought it him,
but upon rocking my tied-down nets,
by the cove, I saw he was nothing,
only a ripple. And my hope engaged
and descended like the turbulent sea
turning into itself, until I turned inland
and pulled the shapeless shawl in

for the walk home. He was the lit moon
who licked my heels, reflected
in the evening's last tidal pools.
I shouldered this weight; perch
flanks for the market, the find
of a washed-up fish net I would rework,
the oysters for dinner and the grainy salt
of one round pearl under my tongue.

A Meditation on Sexuality for Catholic Clergy

Dolores DeLuise

1. "Good"

I once went to confession and lied about committing a sin.

We're having a one-day retreat, a solid day of holy torture, and the six of us, mainly intelligent, mainly Italian American, and mainly uninterested in religion at a Catholic high school womanned by Irish nuns and attended mostly by "good" girls, behave well right through six o'clock mass. When we behave, we're not being "good"; we're just behaving. No matter how much correct behavior we exhibit, we're still not "good," but that's OK. We want to be anything but good. At events like this one, we take our communion with the same nonchalance with which we smoke our cigarettes. We hang out in candy stores and ice cream parlors. The other girls are more sincere, less mature. Being "good" has nothing to do with intelligence or grades; in fact, some of the dumbest are the "goodest." For us, Catholic school is a devil's workshop of wit and laughter.

After breakfast, we are shepherded from place to place in the school for participation in the lectures and prayers that comprise the retreat, and by the time lunch is over, we approach a crucial threshold. We laugh at nothing; I am intoxicated with the absur-

84

dity of the event. Grown people selling us the life to come when we don't even know yet what the present one is about, but are trying hard to find out.

The only man we ever get to see is a middle-aged, short, balding, pot-bellied priest who visits the school a few times a week to teach religion to the senior girls. There is no sign of any other men, not even in administration, but that day we see some exotic-looking priests from a missionary order gliding around the school to help out with the retreat. We cannot believe our eyes when, for a fleeting moment, we behold among them a gorgeous hunk of priest man, an ancient statue come to life, tall with dark hair curling over his collar, and a faint beard that portends a sensuousness we don't understand in the early sixties but can feel in our bellies. A living god exuding sexuality come to save us, with suffering and passion that calls out to us from the depths of his eyes.

Immediately after lunch we are rounded up and assigned to go to confession. Classrooms are set up as confessionals, and we are instructed to select a room and wait on line in the hallway. We stand around, trying to nose out our man's location, when he appears in the hallway, and we zone in on him, following him like lemmings to the classroom he selects; we get on his confession line. We decide to get close to him, right up to him, and maybe turn him on when he hears our sins. The only problem is that we don't have enough sins to warrant spending enough time with him. We need a plan.

Hearts pounding, hormones in overdrive, we plot our moves in hysterical whispers.

"I know," one of us says. "Let's all confess the same sin."

"Yeah." Someone else says, maybe it was me. "A sin about sex."

We're in a huddle. Suggestions fly fast and furious, a litany to the god of pre-penetrative teenage sex.

"What commandment is that again?"

"The seventh commandment!"

"Getting felt up."

"Tongue kissing."

"That's too blunt; say 'French kissing.' "

"You can't say 'felt up' to a priest."

"This is gonna be good."

"What are you gonna say, 'tit'?"

"Grinding?"

"No."

"Humping!"

"That's the same as grinding, stupid."

"No it isn't; you do it lying down."

"When did you ever get to hump?"

"Hurry up; hurry up, it's almost our turn."

"OK. Here it is: Bless me Father for I have sinned. I committed a sin against the seventh commandment and I want to know if French kissing is a mortal sin."

"Claudia—go, go."

She's in there an awful long time. Barbara's next. Finally, Claudia comes out of the room, her olive skin flushed, and Barbara goes in.

"So, so . . . ?"

Before she can answer, Claudia is swept away from us by a nun who instructs her where to go next.

I'm alone in the hall now. Claudia and then Barbara spend a good deal of time at their confessions, but now Joanna, just ahead of me, emerges quickly. I go in. There's no screen between us and I am inches from his mesmerizing profile. On his neck I see a razor cut, a short, straight, thin red line with a pinpoint clump of drying blood in the middle.

"Bless me Father, for I have sinned. I've committed a sin against the seventh commandment, and I want to know—"

"NO. It's not a sin. For your penance, say . . ."

That's it. Confessionis interuptus.

Maybe I should have selected a different commandment. Maybe I should have confessed my true sin: I wasn't "good," but what did that mean, anyway? What commandment did it violate? I was a good student, but I wasn't "good"; I was a virgin, but I wasn't "good." Maybe I shouldn't have lied. Maybe I should have confessed that I was actually in the process of committing the sin of trying to seduce a priest. But was that really a sin, though? Wasn't it really "good" to alert him about the futility of his profession? It was all wrong; why should he serve Jesus when he was himself a god?

That was the last time I lied in order to be close to a man. But that was the first time I thought about the difference between sex and sexuality.

2. Body Geometry

The high school uniform consisted of a maroon jumper, yellow blouse, maroon blazer, maroon and white saddle shoes, bobby socks, *and* stockings. In those days, we held up our stockings with a garter belt, whose very name evokes the Middle Ages. There were no tights, knee-highs, thigh-highs, or pantyhose. Today garter belts are worn only as sexual accessories and during performances, and in both cases more off the body than on—someone finally figured out there's more reason to remove garter belts than to wear them. When I was in high school, they were simply a torture that had to be endured by well-groomed women who wanted to hold up their stockings without rolling them in rubber bands above their knees. Garter belts rode low on your hips, dragged down by the stockings, which were stiff rather than stretchy, cutting into the bony prominences of your pelvis. The metal and rubber mechanisms that held up the stockings scored your thighs. When I peeled them off at night, I heard a "thwunk" as I pulled the rubber out of my flesh.

And then there was the horror of menstruation. Imagine—there was no tampon use for virgins, nor was there an adhesive strip attached to the bottom of the sanitary napkin. The pad had to be attached to an elastic belt and held in place by a metal device with teeth that grasped it. One false or hasty move while attaching would render you, for the duration, the bitten object until you attached a new one. My menstruating body was a map that demonstrated the crisscrossing confinements and interconnectedness of female torture with enough metal on it to interest a dominatrix. I think I was later drawn to heavy metal rockers because their outerwear and their psychic pain reminded me of my own earlier experiences; they screamed and moaned my metallic anguish.

The school wasn't air conditioned but met until the end of June, and those garter belts and stockings became true suffering that we were encouraged to "offer up to Jesus," or "offer up for the suffering souls." I figured I must have sprung quite a few of them out of Purgatory in my time.

The important question, however, was: Why do I have to wear socks *and* stockings? Frankie Avalon had recently informed us that "[w]hen a girl changes from bobby socks to stockings," all sorts of wonderful, new things happen, and I wanted them to happen to me. I was being forced to remain in an ambivalent stage of development, neither pollywog nor frog. Isn't a big, ugly pair of white "bobby socks" pollywog punishment enough? Why did I also have to suffer as a frog? Seniors didn't have to wear bobby socks, but I never made it to that point; among other things, I failed geometry.

Geometry was taught to me by a very small, ruddy, acerbic nun named Sister Mary Dorothy. She said, on the first day of class, that ten of us would fail. I suppose I took that to heart. The Regents exams we practiced on, she said, were 44 percent memorized theorems and 56 percent new material; my grade was a consistent 44. I bore it in silence for the souls in Purgatory.

Toward the end of the spring semester of my sophomore year, I noticed Sister Mary Dorothy had taken to lingering at the bottom of the second floor stairwell, looking up at the girls. It didn't take me long to find out what she was doing there. One hot day, she was able to see up the skirt of my uniform and noticed that I didn't have stockings on. Only bobby socks. This turned out to be an offense even more heinous than failing geometry. Letters and telephone calls ensued.

Right about that time, we were taken on a field trip to the Maryknoll Missionary headquarters, and an item of particular interest pointed out to us was that foot binding had been practiced on Chinese women. We were shown exquisitely ornamented shoes, about four or five inches in length, that fit the mutilated feet of the unfortunate victims. The nuns there were proud of the fact that

Christianity had been in part responsible for ending this horrible torture that rendered upper-class women crippled, unable to walk without assistance. I gazed in horror at the shoes, seemingly constructed of geometric elements, triangles and squares, quite unlike any Western shoes. I was impressed with the Church's proactive stance, but was equally struck by the dissonance implicit in the duality of their vision: We shall not further the confinement of women's bodies in foreign lands because we have so many here at home to work with.

When geometry is applied to their bodies, women do not prosper. I failed geometry repeatedly perhaps because it mirrored the constricting, interconnected shapes made around my waist, hips, thighs, and *mons veneris* by the geometric configurations resulting from the restrictions imposed by my undergarments. Geometry is still a constant reminder that women's business is painful. I will always remain pleased with the 44 percent I had been able to grasp, but continue to resist creating art within the confines of the other 56 percent—the unknown entity I can't fill in because of the constriction and the pain. I have always reached around shapes and numbers to grasp words instead: pliable, open-ended, and bending at my command.

3. Do You Love Jesus?

I don't think I ever got it about Jesus. During hippiedom, when Kris Kristofferson told us that Jesus was "a Capricorn who ate organic food" and we sang "Amazing Grace" with Judy Collins, I connected for some moments with a simple man who looked for astral guidance and espoused inclusive love, as did we all. I still have a fondness for that Jesus. The Jesus I had found at Catholic school, on the other hand, was a dark, enigmatic victim I was encouraged to love unconditionally. Ruling over my life from his place on the cross, pathetic and silent, he reminded me less of a god than of my anguished grammar-school self. It was an ambivalent, uneasy relationship in which we were linked by a heavy chain.

In the third grade, I went from a public school paradise of painting, cutting out, gluing, and printing block letters to a sixty-seven student classroom in Catholic school, presided over by a grim, depressed figure in black, who gave me two weeks to master cursive writing by myself. I didn't think of saying, "No, I can't do that." As a result, I learned something about my own strengths, but my handwriting has always been a stranger to me. Until I got to high school and a different order of nuns, aptly named the Sisters of Mercy, I labored in pain under the shadow of the ever-suffering Jesus, reflecting back my own misery; concurrently and more horrifically, I was subject to the whims of the Sisters of St. Joseph.

A particular spot of hell was the eighth grade, where the fires of the damned were stoked by a Sister Mary Andrea. She was a very good teacher but an ambulatory encyclopedia of kinky pathology. She detested me violently the moment she saw me. It had nothing to do with grades; I was a good student, graduating that year with a 97 percent average, but to her, I wasn't "good." I think she had fantasies about me and delusions about my sexuality, which, at the time, was nonexistent.

The more I tried not to provoke her, the more I seemed to rile her up. The most trivial things transformed her into a raging demon. The brighter part of her personality was a piercing sarcasm. She had a particular issue with my hair, which was thick and longish Italian Other and into which I occasionally wove artificial flowers. She made fun of the way I brushed my hair off my face or held it back while I wrote. The flowers: don't ask.

One day during class she told me that I thought I was a movie star. Furthermore, she said, "The only movie star you resemble is Lassie," who did not, at the moment, need to be replaced. She said this not from the front of the classroom or at her desk, but while perched on the desk of one of the more mature boys, and surrounded by the other mature boys who were the main target of her pedagogy. Classroom discussions took place chiefly among that group of her and about six tall boys with deep voices and pompadours fueled with Brylcream. She began calling me "Lassie."

One day I had left my lunch home, and my brother brought it to my classroom. He found Sister sitting on her usual student desk, crossed the room, and gave it to her. She took the brown bag and said, "Here, Lassie, fetch," throwing the bag across the room at me. It opened, of course, and apple, sandwich, napkins, and celery sticks were strewn about the room. I picked them up off the floor.

During the English Regents exam, a week before graduation, she asked the class to submit to her the mimeographed study sheet she had distributed the week before. I had left mine home and said I would bring it the next day. She became furious. The woman of God, bride of Christ, slapped me across the face and my eyeglasses flew across the room. She made me leave the exam immediately to go home to retrieve the paper. English was my best subject (in which I subsequently earned a PhD), but she forced me to leave the exam so I could "fetch" the mimeographed sheet. She wouldn't let me go during the lunch hour following the exam; it had to be immediately. My mother, at work forty minutes from the house, had to meet me at home to open the door.

This was too much even for my mother, who usually sided with the authorities. She spent an hour on the phone with Mother Superior and Sister. The conversation ended with the threat that I might not graduate the following week. I only got an 89 on my English Regents; I had been looking forward to doing much better, but what amazes me now is that I was able to write anything at all. I attended the graduation ceremony, not knowing until my name was called whether or not it actually would be.

At the end of my sophomore year of high school, not only had I failed geometry, but I had also failed my second year of Latin. I was ready to go back to public school to do the high school equivalent of drawing, cutting, and pasting. My mother, however, had made some kind of geometry deal for me, and if I passed Latin over the summer, they would take me back in the fall for my junior year.

The teacher I had for summer school was named Sister Mary Dolores, and, I've always thought "Dolores" was her alter-ego, and that her name was probably a good Irish Kathleen or so. I probably was the exotic other she really wanted to be, and she hated me on sight. She was the only nun I had trouble with in high school, sarcastic, picking on me at every opportunity—shades of

Sister Mary Andrea, to whom she bore a marked resemblance. I was convinced, in fact, that they were sisters: same features, build, and timbre of voice. Our toxic relationship proved terminal.

I had a boyfriend that summer who was a Marine. He was Jewish and his name was Barry, another exotic other. I think she heard me talking about him—the anti-Christ, God forbid—to one of my classmates because her antennae visibly perked up when we talked about boyfriends during breaks.

Once, toward the end of the summer, she called on me and I was having trouble answering. I was wearing Barry's gargantuan high school ring on a chain around my neck, and nervously slid it back and forth on the chain as I consulted my notes in an attempt to answer. She burst out forcefully and hatefully, looming above me just as I was figuring out the answer: *"You love that ring more than you love Jesus!"*

If I had been a teenager of the current generation, I would have said, "Duh . . ." but I had no such vocabulary. I was flabbergasted that she had actually said something so irrelevant; I simply couldn't grasp the concept.

I began to laugh. I laughed hysterically and uncontrollably for quite a few minutes. A celestial lightness permeated my body. My spirit was free. Not only did I not love Jesus as much as I loved the ring, or, more precisely, kind of loved Barry, but my ambivalence about Jesus was cleared up at that moment: I had never loved Jesus at all. Ever. Just as I had never loved my Catholic grammar school self. In that miraculous, liberating moment it was clearly revealed to me that I didn't have to—I had left them both behind forever. I was suddenly and completely released, physically and emotionally, from Catholic schools and from suffering at the hands of the strange women who worked in them.

I turned down the geometry deal because all I could forecast for my future was New Utrecht Public High School. No more Latin. No more geometry. No more Jesus. No more crimes to commit just by being myself. Hello, General Studies, here I come.

Moth Song

Sarah Colona

Mother told me
Good girls die first
Pass in their sleep
Wake beside God

Those clever girls
Marry for love
Make few mistakes
Have no regrets

My priest told me
Bad girls die last
Watch good friends go
Then die alone

Those wicked girls
Hunger for love
Give in too quick
Relive their sins

This one question
(I never asked
Either of them)
I put to God

Is the singed moth
Denied entrance
Or does a scar
Strengthen her prayer?

Last of the Tomboy Pings

Patti See

Two o'clock on a Saturday afternoon, and my husband and son have been gone three hours. J. is with his wife and kids, so I've got the phone book out to look up old friends. Not loneliness but getting used to being alone brings a rush of panic for me. By the time my friends arrive it will be gone, and I will play the hostess they expect of me.

After my calls I see my next door neighbor in her yard. Since Harvey died Ingrid has taken on his jobs with a vengeance, speed mowing the lawn and cleaning up after her Rottweilers twice a week.

Harvey disappeared a month ago. Good neighbors bring food with babies and death, but I didn't know what to do when one's gone missing. Each night my husband Jack carried over steaming crock pots of Sloppy Joes or hot dishes to feed a dozen men who gathered around Ingrid's patio in the early evening. Search parties covered a hundred mile radius, tips came in from two states away, but still no one had seen a forty-year-old, crew-cutted man with "Dog Eat Dog" tattooed across the fading Rottweiler on his chest.

I secretly hoped that Harvey found a hot babe somewhere, maybe wearing a straw hat like the one he liked on me, ditched his identity along the way and simply rode off on his Harley. On the fourth night Jack and I watched a squad car pull in next door and heard howls so woefully mammalian they could only be a woman's.

Harvey was found in a ditch. He spun out going just twenty miles an hour on a country road, but his motorcycle dragged him and snapped his neck.

I watch for Ingrid in our adjoining yards or wait for her shadow late at night in her upstairs window. I am intrigued by what a woman does without the man she's lived with for twenty years. I haven't spoken to her since Harvey's memorial service. She wore a cowgirl outfit somewhere between *Annie Get Your Gun* and *Debbie Does Dallas*: red western boots, denim skirt, and a frilly blouse cut so low it looked laced into her breasts.

When Jack and I first married, I used to imagine my own widow's outfit—black satin dress and pillbox hat. I decided recently that perhaps my pain of losing Jack and Sam, in a plane crash or car wreck, is less than the pain my leaving will cause them. Being home alone gives me time to consider how their hearts will break differently: a boy who thinks he's done something wrong, a man who knows he has.

"Hey," I say to Ingrid across the yard.

"Ahhk, Tessa," Ingrid says, cigarette wedged in one side of her mouth, plastic pooper scooper in her hand. Her broad face with its soft features makes her German accent and deep voice more surprising. You expect the nose-twitching *Bewitched* cuteness of Samantha Stevens, you get the harshness of Rocky and Bullwinkle's Natasha. "How are you surviving with your boys off to Boy Scout camp?"

"It's Cub Scouts. Sam is too little for Boy Scouts." I walk toward her fence. "It's weird being home alone," I say, more honestly than I expect. "I was just thinking that I've never been home without either of them before. I still hear Sam, like he's a room away. I miss him already."

"Jack told me it's only three days," she says.

"You're right." I can be the most self-absorbed person in the world: I know they're coming back, and I'll be waiting. I tell her, "I'm having some friends over tonight, come over for a beer."

"You bet," she says with Rottweilers on either side of her.

I have known my guests since we were six—Dawne, Tammy, and Mona. We endured twelve years of Catholic school together and continue to gather a few times a year. A decade after high school, none of us is good or bad enough to hate. I'm surprised when Ingrid lets herself in my porch door an hour after they arrive. She cackles at Mona's story about a classroom of ninth graders mumbling quietly in Sister Mary Simon's reading class until she turned up the volume on her hearing aid. Though Ingrid is fifteen years older than my friends and me—and from another country—we have nuns in common.

"Sister must have been seventy-five years old when we knew her," I say. "She was nearly deaf and blind, but she taught me to be a reader."

We tell drinking stories, highlights of our rebellious youth. We were so caught up in just saying no to drugs that we spent much of high school lost in an alcohol haze. Ingrid laughs at all of our stories, and we laugh as though we've never heard them before. Time has a way of giving us back to ourselves: funnier, smarter, goofier, better.

"And how many dead brain cells?" Tammy says, a nurse's response.

Dawne says, "I just heard about a new study that said only the weakest brain cells are damaged by drugs and alcohol, the ones that would die anyway." She takes a long swill from her beer for effect.

"Nothing worse that a fifteen-year-old Catholic girl can do than skip school and get drunk in a park," someone says, maybe Ingrid.

We didn't know then how much worse it could get, I want to say.

After Ingrid leaves to walk her dogs, Mona says, "I kissed someone besides my husband." The way she says the words in one breath means she's been holding this news in a long time, or, knowing Mona, since last night.

"Don't tell your husband," Tammy says.

"Duh," Mona says.

We are able to be sixteen again, the four of us alone together. Tammy plays with her hair. Mona cracks her knuckles as she talks. The last time I went out with them, Tammy and Mona looked middle-aged to me. It's their outfits—slacks and sweaters for every occasion—or their dispositions. Though we're almost thirty, I still picture Dawne as a twelve-year-old with a sweatband around her head, another tomboy like me. She's been my best friend since grade school, and I may always see the girl in her eyes.

Now Dawne slouches. I blow bubbles between drags on my cigarette.

Mona says, "It's not like I wanted to sleep with him."

"Adultery is never just about sex," Dawne says.

"I just wanted to kiss him so I did. That's that. Why does everything have to mean something to you guys? I know Tessa's messed up that way, but when did she get to you two?"

"What planet are you on?" Tammy says. "You kissed someone who's not your husband and you think it might NOT mean something?" She laughs. We've all had too much to drink to be talking about this.

"I just wanted to feel that again," Mona says, "a ping in my stomach when I kiss a guy, not a husband but a real guy who's kissing me not because he wants to sleep with me in the next three minutes or wants me to iron his shirt, but because he just wants to kiss me because I'm cute."

"You're right," Dawne says, "that really doesn't mean anything."

"How long have you been married?" I ask.

Tammy interrupts, "Back up the bus." She gets a little loopy when she drinks wine. "Ping? What's a ping?"

We all talk at once. "A tickle belly," Dawne says. "A flutter in your cooch," Mona says. "Arousal," I say.

"Oh," Tammy says. "A Mary Jane. My grandmother called it that when we drove out in the country on hilly roads. Ping, huh? No—it's a Mary Jane."

Dawne says to Mona, "You need to get over this ping and realize if you're going to be with a guy for a long time you don't get butterflies in your stomach or wherever. It just doesn't happen like it happened." She lights a cigarette. "When you were in high school. Or whenever."

I go inside for another bottle of wine and return with a recent birthday present, a baseball cap with PING in large black letters across the front. I toss it on the table.

Mona snatches the hat with both hands. "Where did you get this?" she asks. She still thinks it's her word, and I've never met anyone else who calls arousal that.

Dawne says, "The golf company. The hat is a golfing accessory." Dawne and Mona fight over the hat and finally take turns trying it on.

"Let Tammy wear it first," I say. "She needs a real ping after all of those Mary Janes."

I watch Ingrid return her dogs to their kennel. I want her to come back, to referee or to hear more of our stories. She goes into her house without looking toward my porch.

An hour or so later, the table cluttered with empty beer cans and wine bottles, someone gets the idea after everyone talking at once that the only way any of us can speak is to put on my PING hat and raise our hands. We regress to two tomboys and two girly-girls shooting our hands to the ceiling like we've really got the answers. We bring with us to this table everyone we have ever loved or wanted to, three marriages, six pregnancies, four children, three counselors.

Tammy goes first. She adjusts the hat and sips her wine.

"Once I dreamt I was masturbating with an apple," Tammy says.

"Granny Smith or Pink Lady?" I ask. Everyone laughs but no one can acknowledge me without the hat.

"I dreamt I was masturbating with a Dee-licious apple," Tammy continues, "and I kept taking bites out of it. It was really erotic, especially telling Max about it in the morning."

We all wail. When we quiet down, Mona says, "Max sounds like a sensitive guy."

Dawne raises her hand high above her head and waves it in the air. Only Tammy can call on her. Tammy looks around, like Sister Mary Simon used to do, nose in the air, seeing none of us or all of us in a blur.

Finally she points at Dawne and says, "The fine looking, big breasted woman in the front row." She hands over the hat.

Dawne says, "I was sixteen or so and this guy drove me out to a cornfield after a party. He stopped his truck and sat back in his seat, looked over at me like with this totally fake soap opera face and said—" Dawne laughs. "He said, *Will you make love to me.* Can you imagine? I told him no, of course. His bumper sticker was something like *Honk if you love NASCAR,* and he tries this sensitive line. It would have been different if he said *I want to jump your bones.*"

I laugh even though I've heard this story before. For the first time I wonder if Dawne tells it because she regrets saying no. Or worse, has she had anyone since *ask* her so tenderly? She's lived with her boyfriend Wayne on and off since high school, more out of convenience than anything. They have two kids together.

Mona's hand has been up while Dawne finished her story. Dawne takes her time calling on her, looks around, and continues to talk.

"Stupid things we do when we're girls," Dawne says, looking from Tammy to me to Mona and back to me. "Led by that ping and all. Thinking that ping is the main thing."

Finally she settles on Mona. "The average looking chick in the back row with the hoop earrings and summer slacks."

Mona pulls her ponytail through the back of the PING hat. "I was dating these two guys once and I was in bed with one of them and the other guy showed up at my apartment. It's like looking back at another person, like it was some wild woman who wasn't even me."

I want to tell her that's my life now. I nod along with the others.

Everyone knows it's my turn; I'm the only one left. I have stories I can't tell, stories they would never believe happened to Tessa Lam.

I raise my hand high, not because I'm eager to answer, but because raising my hand is so fun. I don't remember the last time I reached to the ceiling, waved an arm so eagerly it might fall off at the elbow.

Mona calls on me immediately, "The formerly gold star on her forehead girl, in, of course, the front row." I am not the drunkest here.

I motion toward my chest. She adds, "With the perky nubbins."

I'm so wrapped up in getting called on, that I forget I have to say something. A hundred miles away my husband and son are telling campfire stories, maybe even some of mine, with the other Cub Scouts. I am struck by how much I miss them.

I tell a story from a book I'm reading. "I was with this guy once in college and whenever he ejaculated he yelled, *Ouch*. Like he just stubbed his toe."

"Who?" Dawne asks. She thinks she knows all of my stories. It's not her turn but I answer.

"Just a guy I knew in college. Some guy. No name. You didn't give a name."

"Mine was a real person," she says. She knows I make friends with characters I read about, sometimes more intimately than with real people.

"You are so weird," Mona says to me.

I adjust the PING hat, which feels more like a dunce cap once it's actually on.

"Okay, okay," I say. "I was seven months pregnant and worried about losing all muscle tone in my vagina after having a baby."

Christ, what's the connection to this story, one I forgot I even had? I hear Ingrid in my head, saying, *Ahhk Tessa, the fear of losing the ping*. She sounds the way Freud does in movies.

I say, "Actually I had this idea that if I did enough Kegel exercises and sit-ups, I'd be able to force that baby out with no pain. So for months I did Kegels everywhere: driving in the car, sitting in church. I got so good that no one could tell I was flexing *those* muscles. One night I was taking a bath, doing my Kegels as usual. Jack didn't want to have sex once I hit that eight month mark, so all he would do is pleasure me in other ways. That night after my bath I thought I was coming and coming. Until Jack stopped, raised his head above my belly so I could see him and said, *You taste like bath water*."

My friends squeal. "There's a keeper," Dawne says. I don't know if she means my husband or the story.

Tammy says slowly, "He drank your bath water?"

"It's not like it was a test," I say. Tammy raises her hand.

I say to her, "Lovely young woman in the GAP cotton sweater."

Tammy says, "You guys know I've never had a healthy relationship with a man." She holds the hat and looks around the table.

I want to say, *Has any of us,* but it's not my turn. No one I know lives the way I do.

The more I drink, the louder Ingrid speaks to me, as Freud, again. *You've already left him with your heart,* Ingrid says. I twist the hat around my finger. I say, "I have a lover."

"Tessa," Dawne says, "I think we're done hearing stories, don't you?"

"Whatever," Mona says. "You read too much. Like Tessa Lam would ever sleep with anyone but her husband." She laughs. "You don't have to try to top me. When are you going to grow up?"

"You caught me," I say.

Later I embrace Mona and then Tammy in front of my porch door. Dawne lingers at the table until we hear their cars backing out of my driveway. She says she's sleeping over and doesn't wait for my response. It's 3:30 in the morning. Dawne talks as she picks up empty bottles. "You know if you tell Mona anything, within twenty-four hours half of Downeville will know what's going on with you."

I nod. My life had been so dull for so many years that I couldn't imagine anyone gossiping about me.

Dawne and I walk to my bedroom. I pull back my comforter, and we both stand looking at the bed, waiting for each other to choose her spot. We've shared a bed since first grade, though I can't remember our last sleepover. We each lay hugging one side of my mattress, the expanse of my queen-sized bed between us.

Dawne turns on her side and props her head in one hand, elbow against my pillow. I can almost see her eyes.

"I think I understand about him," Dawne says. "He gave you that PING hat, didn't he? You might be the last person in the world who really believes in the ping. Not like Mona, but really believes."

"Now I'm the last of the goddamn Mohicans? Sister Mary Simon would be so proud."

Dawne laughs. She says, "If I had someone like that in my life I wouldn't give a second thought to leaving."

My stomach flutters. I have so much to say to her that only sleep will do right now.

Penance

Donna J. Gelagotis Lee

The panel slid over with a thump.
Which priest did God choose for her?
She began, trying to see who it was,
but then a voice sterner than God's
pronounced her penance. She left
with haste, hurrying to the pew to cross
herself, angry at *who does he think he is?*
scolding her with contrition as long
as a sermon. She had to get back
home, go biking with her friend, listen to
records. Next time she'll come early, wait
to see which priest enters which box. She'll
stand in the line that's faster, listen to the voice
that's gentler, say a few Hail Marys—that's
all she'll have to do.

Thou Shalt Not Have Strange Gods Before Me

Pamela Galbreath

I looked them straight in the eyes, those severe Apostles perched in their alcoves along the long hall from Mother Superior's office to the playground door. With mustered audacity, I whisper-shouted, "See? I am a good Catholic child of God!" But Saint Peter's two fingers, poised to begin the Sign of the Cross, caught my eye, humbled me.

Bowing my head obediently, I ran past them all, loving the echo of my steps on the marble floor. I held in my excited giggle and pushed open the door to the playground where my sixth-grade girlfriends, thinking I'd been called in for knuckle-striking punishment, waited. Posture proud, voice triumphant, I imitated Mother Superior's voice. Imagining her minty breath: "I am giving you the Blessed Virgin card, Pamela, for always saying 'I'll try,' for never saying 'I can't.'" Wasn't this just as good as the moment when the burning Saint Joan of Arc turned her eyes upward, saw and spoke to the vision of Jesus?

The jealous girls swarmed, grabbing for the laminated holy card, the largest and most beautiful any sixth-grade girl had received this year. On the front, the Blessed Virgin Mary stood on a small globe against a cumulous sky, her blue robes aswirl, tiny gold stars forming her halo. On the back, the Hail Mary—Oh, I had done superbly, for the text was in Latin: Ave Maria, gratia plena—and Mother Superior had instructed me: "The prayer will protect you from danger if you pray it repeatedly." Her eyes, distorted behind her wire-rimmed glasses, left an impression. Catholicism would eventually fade from my life, but the Hail Mary would remain a secret, silent prayer of hopeful, desperate resort.

I finally let the card pass from friend to friend and relived the details of the escort to Mother Superior's office by a novitiate in an aproned habit, wisps of hair slightly exposed under starched white veil, tiny laced leather shoes clicking on the floor. I plodded behind her in the wool coat my mother insisted I would grow into, my brown plaid dress hanging below my knees, white ankle socks disappearing into the heels of my saddle Oxfords, my skinny legs just beginning to sprout black hairs. I desired the novitiate's tailored, cinched profile and wished her vows of obedience to the Order would someday be my own.

Mother Superior welcomed me, placing a warm, pudgy hand on my head. Judging the warmth a miracle, I eagerly kissed the gold band on her left ring finger, signifying that she was a bride of the Church. My head remained bowed, though, for this was the same Mother Superior who, only two weeks earlier, had blown into the girls' bathroom, skirts swooshing and shoes pounding, and bellowed at our little crowd for staying to "vainly appreciate our reflections in the mirrors" for too long.

What would her anger have been like had she known we were trying our best to make sense of the movie shown in Health class—a woman's soft, pleasant voice explaining, for those of us who would not be called by God to his service, preparation for the blessing of motherhood, the script leaving huge gaps for our imaginations to fill. In single file, we left the bathroom, reciting in unison the Act of Contrition.

"I wish I could trade you," said Mary Ann, her eyes distorted behind thick glasses. "Look, I have Saint Agnes and Saint Cecelia." The other girls, clutching the cards they had brought to trade, waited for my response.

Our rewards at St. Mary's in Alexandria, Virginia, were always holy cards of the female saints. We were hypnotized by the female martyrs' boyish bodies and faces, their tortuous deaths brought on by their devotion to Jesus, blood pouring from their wounds, their eyes raised toward Heaven. They had died for the tall, dark, handsome Jesus, sexy with his long hair and gentle eyes. We yearned for the cards of those saints who had died the bloodiest deaths: St. Agnes, beheaded at age fourteen; St. Agatha, whose breasts were chopped off; St. Catherine, turned on a spiked wheel and then, when the wheel broke, beheaded; and my favorite, St. Cecelia, who lingered in obedient agony for three days after her head was partially severed. Clutching the cards of these martyrs to our hearts, excited by their androgynous, dramatic images, we vowed that we too would die for Jesus.

"Nope, sorry," I said, skipping away, my card at my chest, angling close to the playground-duty Sisters, who smiled and nodded. The Blessed Virgin, who knew the passion of her son's death on the cross, was mine now. I hadn't told my friends how Mother Superior had patted my shoulders, how from that day forward I wanted only to wear the habit and veil, to dedicate my life entirely to the Sisters and the Blessed Heart of Jesus. A fervent prepubescent, I vowed to embrace this decision forever, like an obedient child and potential martyr.

On the Saturday before Easter, only three months after receiving the Blessed Virgin's card and pledging my life to her, I awoke and instead of pondering Jesus's resurrection, I could focus only on my new Easter purse on the dresser. Seeing it made me giddy.

My mother had surprised me with the purse. It was everything I wanted: purple and lavender flowers embroidered on white linen, a strap of gold links that could be hidden for the "clutch" effect. With the purse came short cotton gloves, white lace-edged dress socks, and black patent leather pumps with—now I was no longer a child!—one inch heels. And then, from tissue paper wrapping, she whisked out a beautiful dress of sky blue fabric, its white scalloped collar and cuffs adorned with tiny blue buttons. A full skirt flared from—I had waited so long for this—a fitted waist and belt.

"Want Mommy to get you dressed?"

I was a sixth grader now, but I did not think to protest the daily ritual of my mother pulling off my jammies and slipping on my white cotton underwear. This morning, though, she pushed her finger against my left breast and said, "Those breasts are going to need a bra."

Breasts. She had said it. I had breasts. I was becoming a woman—and my mother was dressing me. I pulled away, announced, "I want to get dressed myself."

"Now, now, you don't need to be silly. Two cotton T shirts will hide them." With that, my mother stood me up and went to the closet. Would my breasts upset Mother Superior?

On Easter Sunday, I carried my new purse to Mass. To make it look full, I first stuffed it with Kleenex, then added the saints cards I'd recently received for perfect spelling, a meticulously printed assignment, no absences for a month, confession and communion every Sunday during Lent, and for raising my hand—the only one in the class—when Sister Ignatius asked who not only *owned* but also *used* a holy water fountain. Just before I left my room, I slid open a dresser drawer, and from under my clothing, removed the gold case of blood red lipstick that my best friend Ann had stolen from her mother and given to me, and slipped it into the bottom of my purse.

The two front pews were engorged with heavy black bodices, skirts, veils, stockings, and shoes. The Sisters, even the sweet, young ones who often let me curl into the folds of their billowy skirts, had become two black caterpillars, undulating and pulsating as they made the Sign of the Cross, knelt, struck their breasts with tight fists during the *Mea Culpa,* brought their rosary crucifixes to their pale lips, readying themselves to receive Jesus's body and blood. Sister Karen Marie, the science teacher who shared every year the story of a former student who got an infection and died from squeezing her pimples, had told us of caterpillars in South America that fed on flesh. I was relieved that my father steered us toward our usual pew far in the back of the church.

Inhaling the lingering scent of Good Friday's incense, I hoped the Sisters would not turn around to see us. They would not approve of the gold chain on my purse catching the light of the church's chandeliers, or my gorgeous new dress with its cinched waist. During the drive to church, I hadn't been able to stop sliding the soft, shiny taffeta of the skirt along the insides of my thighs.

~

The next autumn saw a ritual, the seeds of which were nurtured over the summer by taffeta, lavender on linen, and the skin of my thighs. After dinner, announcing tons of homework, I slipped from the dinner table to my bedroom, closed the door, pulled books from my school bag, and opened them, in case my mother came in. From my pencil case, I removed three folded *Life* magazine pictures of John Fitzgerald Kennedy, and laid them on my bedspread. My handsome, sexy president was younger than a president should be—with tousled hair, his narrow black tie a little off-center, he was positively accessible to a skinny, shy Catholic girl with frizzy hair and straight As. In one picture, he wore a tuxedo and smiled at Jackie, who was dressed in satin and pearls, her hair swept back with glittery barrettes. My mother once explained, while yanking a comb through my hair, that the First Lady also had naturally curly hair and perhaps, with work, someday mine might look like hers. I wasn't jealous of Jackie. I believed the two of us could share Jack. I knew she too was shy, and had been, still was, a good Catholic girl.

Cross-legged on the bed, I pulled the pictures onto my lap and imagined being in the president's arms. I thought of kissing his picture, but in a giggly blush, I refrained. Drawn as I was to his perfect self—I, like so many others, was ignorant of his philandering and his debilitating illnesses—I certainly had not crossed over to full carnal delight. Not yet.

Ann and I spent every recess on the asphalt playground talking about the president. The high chain link fence and the Sisters protected us from the out-of-work derelicts of Alexandria who wandered past, paper-bagged bottles concealed in their wide coat pockets, stopping to stare at the young girls who still loved to skip, the fronts of their skirts flipping up. We were not unaware of these men. We found them interesting.

Ann's mother gave us her movie magazines, and we cut out every picture of JFK. We had to keep secret from the Sisters our adoration of the president, so we passed his pictures folded under holy cards. Lately, we didn't care which holy cards.

Their own sexuality may have been suppressed, but the Sisters certainly knew ours was blooming. They patrolled the cafeteria, their hands tucked beneath the starched white bodices over which bounced their gold crucifixes, their suspicious eyes steady on us. We murmured our Grace After Meals until they glided past. Then, leaning our heads together, lightheaded with the thrill, we slid to each other the weeks' magazine booty—new pictures of President Kennedy, concealed under the random holy cards. Ann, far ahead of the rest of us in sexual knowledge, whispered that she had propped the president's picture on her dresser and then touched herself *there*. At that moment, I thought Ann the most amazing girl in all of God's kingdom, but that night, in contrition, I prayed the Rosary twice. Once for her. Once for me, for having listened.

On November 22, 1963, a Friday, classes were dismissed early to attend the weekly "Getting to Know You" Club in the auditorium. The Sisters shared wonderful stories about their vocation, called to the service of *our* Father, called to be *His* bride. After the stories, we knelt to pray to God for instruction in choosing this same vocation.

As we sang "Michael Rowed the Boat Ashore," accompanied by Sister Agnes on guitar, Father Simon entered. The music ceased. He stepped onto the lower stage.

"President John F. Kennedy," and at the name, there was a stir like shallow, quick breathing, "our Catholic president, has been shot in Dallas, Texas." The stir turned into shrieks.

Sister Agnes snapped, "Girls, shame on you! Pay attention to Father." Silence.

Father continued. "This is a good time for us to examine our own consciences. Kneel and pray with me for President Kennedy's soul which, if he dies, will linger in Purgatory."

Purgatory? My president in purgatory? Why wouldn't John Fitzgerald Kennedy's soul go *straight* to Heaven? I *hated* Father for saying that. Then, picturing an empty White House, a world with no more pictures of my president, I started to cry.

The room knelt in one movement. Father swept his hand nonchalantly from head to heart to shoulders, "In the name of the Father, and of the Son, and of the Holy Ghost." My friends and I bowed our heads but didn't pray. Instead, we whispered our fears through clasped hands: Would he live? Was Jackie okay? When I pictured her holding the wounded president in her arms, an unfamiliar warm sensation rose in my body. I leaned into the girl next to me and hissed the prayer we'd been taught, with one defiant, sacrilegious change: "*President Kennedy,* in my head, on my lips, in my heart."

While I waited, exhausted from grief, with my older sister on the school steps for our mother to arrive, my panties suddenly felt damp. During the trip to our grandparents' house in Maryland, where we would spend Thanksgiving week, I sat sideways on the back seat so I wouldn't dampen the station wagon's new upholstery. Walter Cronkite's words played over and over: "From Dallas, Texas, the flash—apparently official—President Kennedy died at one p.m. Central Standard Time, two p.m. Eastern Standard Time, some thirty-eight minutes ago. Vice President Johnson has left the hospital in Dallas, but we do not know to where he has proceeded. Presumably, he will be taking the oath of office shortly, and become the thirty-sixth President of the United States."[1] Leaning against the cold car door, I cried quietly for the end of Camelot, for the end of my first romance. I wondered how I had peed in my pants without knowing.

As we entered with our suitcases, the television blared, repeating the black-and-white blur of the Dealey Plaza motorcade, Jackie's pink suit and pillbox hat, LBJ taking the oath of office on Air Force One. There were no pictures of the president, his skull, his blood—only sterilized commentary. I went into my grandmother's bathroom, pulled down my panties and saw a circle of brown-red blood. When I peed, the bowl filled with redness. I gingerly pulled up my damp panties, shivering at the sticky wetness, went to the bedroom where my sister and I would sleep, and called for Mother. Riveted to the television screen, she sent my sister. Debbie pulled her own sanitary belt, a Kotex pad, and a pair of panties from her suitcase. I followed her back to the bathroom. "You don't have cramps?" she asked as she showed me how to put on the pad. "Just wait, you will. That's why it's called *the curse.*"

Through the long November night of Walter Cronkite's sad voice, I found solace in the warm drips of blood from inside of me, the heavy grief that I knew Jackie and I shared, my womanhood.

∼

In the early spring of 1964, Camelot was just a memory. Lyndon Johnson, now established in the presidency, looked to us girls like an old dog. New royalty, the Beatles, had emerged. The Sisters strictly forbade Beatle worship. No talk. No songs. No books. No magazines. No cards. "They entice sexuality and break the First Commandment," Sister Mary Immaculé explained, "and neither Jesus nor the Virgin Mary would want that, girls." We nodded sincerely, but the pull was too great. We mock-chanted as we increased our cache of Beatle paraphernalia: "I *am* the *Lord* thy *God*. Thou *shalt* have no *strange* gods be-*fore* me." At Ann's house, we wore the red lipstick.

A single package of flat pink gum could yield up to four Beatle cards, depending on the brand. The cards exuded a sugary smell until our fondling made it fade. We conducted our Beatle card trading in the farthest corner of the chain link fence, or in the small church cemetery that separated the girls' and boys' playgrounds.

In the cemetery, we were to follow a strict, respectful vow of silence. We were to use our time there only to pray for the poor souls still in purgatory or, worse, in limbo. Disobedience brought the ruler down hard on our knuckles or shoulder blades. The punishment was worth it, though. Huddled in groups of two, we resumed our soft chatter as the groups of playground-duty Sisters moved on. We handed off the precious cards of John, Paul, George, and Ringo under our steno assignment pads where dictated prayers had once been carefully penned. Dipping behind memorial obelisks, we tangled ourselves in larger groups and softly sang, "Goin' to the chapel and we're gonna get marr-ar-arried." Then, contemptuous of the Sisters who professed that *they* loved us, we practiced, on each other, kissing on the lips.

By day, I hid my stash of forty cards in the bottom of my book bag, at night, under my blankets. One night, I lined up ten cards of George Harrison, my favorite, along my inner thigh, pressed my legs together and slept. The next morning, the cards were buckled from my sweat, nearly ruined. Using words I had recently learned, I cursed my stupidity.

My sister sold me a magazine picture of George. He slumped in an upholstered chair, holding a bottle of beer, looking sullen, rebellious, sexy, his long legs spread wide apart. My daydreams about George were vivid, intense—the lurid daydreams of a miserably naive girl still under the spell of the Blessed Virgin and the Sisters who spoke of their allegiance to Jesus with uncomplicated, reassuring authority.

Carrying George's picture in my plaid pencil pouch wasn't enough. I started slipping it out at dangerous moments to breathe in his image. During catechism class. In the dimly lit confessional, where I fervently admitted my sins and begged for forgiveness. During prayers to Jesus and the Blessed Virgin. Unleashed, I knew I had to hide George. Worried that my mother might find him, I sought where she no longer went: the top drawer of my dresser, in a nest of panties. I quietly closed the drawer.

That Monday, the Sisters swept angrily through our lockers, through our book bags, through our purses, in search of anything Beatles. Before closing my locker door, Mother Superior smiled once more at the Blessed Virgin card, propped on my top metal shelf, and patted my head. "Good girl," she said, as I stood proudly. Her breath was stale.

Note

1. Excerpt from Walter Cronkite's CBS broadcast on November 22, 1963, from Walter Cronkite, *A Reporter's Life* (New York: Alfred A. Knopf, 1996).

Sister No One

Liz Dolan

After a devilish ex beau, Johnny Noone, sent me
a mock Daily News, headlines prating
Bronx Chorus Girl Enters Convent
my postulant mistress excoriated me
her thin lip sticking to her teeth
as she spewed forth syllables like a printing press,
Tell your friend, Mr. No One,
he could at least have the decency to sign his name.

But Sister, his name is Noone.
Like the ink on a newspaper left
in the rain I, nineteen,
was the one who was disappearing.
My face sour-white like a millstone
I scratched the rule like a hair shirt,
chewed Aquinas like succulent pork,
wallowed in the freedom of poverty
a Dominican Dresden doll goose-stepping to rubrics:
custody of the eyes, no particular friendships
Magna Silencia. In the refectory,

black-gowned and lisle-stockinged,
I beheld my own shallows in pans
of boiling water I ferried on trays to the end
of each oblong table for the professed to wash
their plates with a cauliflower wand,
another cog in the wheel of medieval efficiency.

When late I prostrated myself on the chapel floor
made the venia, mea culpa, mea culpa, and kissed the cold tiles.

Superstitions of a Catholic Childhood

Martha K. Grant

i.

Chiseled glass beads
rest in a nest of cotton
she'll save for later,
scrubbing pink polish
from chewed
nails. Her new rosary
is snug in its box.

She understands it has no
spiritual value yet,
unblessed—
still a generic strand
of metal links, faux
crystal, and a machine-
pressed Jesus, soldered
to a tin cross prettied up
with dainty filigree
for girlish hands.

She will take it to the priest.

She will stand
in practiced
reverence, shifting
from one small saddle oxford
to the other; she will count
the decades of precise
black buttons,
perfectly spaced,
trailing sorrowful
mysteries,
neck to hem,
down the front
of his long cassock,
as he gathers the beads
into his left palm.

He is careful to place
the cross on top,
the tin Jesus face up.

She will hold
her breath, watching
his flattened right hand
(cuticles and nails gnawed)
transcribing its own cross
in the air above
her pale pink
future
prayers.

ii.

She will report, as instructed,
to the rectory door,
waiting on the wooden porch,
shifting (again)

from one anxious foot
to the other,
the harsh buzzer
jarring sharply;

she will press it
just once—
quickly—

wanting no one
to answer . . .
not wanting.

Wanting.

iii.

The red floral pattern
in the drapes,
the slant of midday
(school day) sun
through tilted blinds
striping his office wallpaper,
the scratchy texture
of green desk blotter
on bare bottom. . . .

You will learn to like it,
his low voice ringing
in her ear,
for years.

iv.

*I would think your sense
of modesty . . .*
her mother will say
to the young teenager,

her words trailing off—
a proper woman's
abbreviated version
of Sex Ed, as though
(modesty, above all)
no more need be said.

She was right—
there was no more
to say. It was
too late,

about eight years
too late.

V.

Making rounds,
he will visit her
after a teenage surgery.

Unaccustomed
to being a patient,
(self-conscious
in a hospital gown),
she will not know
what to say,
what social niceties
might be expected.

Accustomed
to being a priest,
he will suggest:
Would you like my blessing?

She will feel remiss,
chastised—

she should have thought
to ask. Didn't she know
better?

Yes, Father.

She will feel embarrassed—
not holier
or healthier—
when he leaves.

Fear and Trembling

Lauren K. Alleyne

After Kierkegaard

And there are many ways to come undone
—some more exquisite than others. Ask Eve,
she will tell you apple-lust unwrapped her
left her cold and with a word for *shiver.*
Lot's wife is witness that a backward glance
is enough—nostalgia pillared her. But,
I imagine the somewhat greater deeds:
the Red Sea unstitched like a turquoise braid;
the lion's den, its many hungry mouths;
Isaac's bewildered screams: *why, daddy, why?*
And what terrible choice to peel back doubt
like a bandage, without question or lack
to say *Here am I,* to renounce relief:
step in, seize the knife, and to know belief.

Rewinding the Wedding Tape

Patti See

The seventh anniversary gift is wool.
I taste it after our wedding tape tradition
when I stay to rewind alone.
Everyone dances off the altar
and I can't hear the *man and wife*
our priest says that in marriage
a schoolboy and waitress become.

In reverse every notion of ceremony
is a motion away, an easy glimpse
of undoing as they return
their rings to the bearer,
the groom's lips un-vowing
the reverted bride's left idle.
They hobble up the aisle.

Walking backwards no one can bear
to lead, her trousseau becomes
an untied knot of satin and lace
the eight foot veil is more a waiting
shroud ungathered like this by attendants.
Chaplin in borrowed shoes, the groom
steps back to rescind his bride.

There's me as I remember me
unhanded by a snare of roses
just for a moment at this inverted
beginning, my new end,
wedged between parents and two exits
given back to myself.

Invisible Nature

Leonore Wilson

My good shrink names off a trombone of new medicines with their capacity for change. This is her form of devotion, her creed of repetition, to cure my wound, to rid me of half a century of sorrow, pain, and anger as if to leave no trace or shadow of my former self—the one on fire, the Medea who doesn't reason, the one filled with the tyranny of things. This angel's a sleuth, says it's "her duty" to make me well, to make me whole, as if hauling me back to memory's garden, before I tasted the black bread of rebellion, before rebellion whispered, "come hither," for what I feel she says, *I feel too much.* On the path to "healing," I've tried thirteen elixirs. Thirteen's enough.

I married at twenty. By twenty-three I had a handful of babies. I said I would not be like my mother, I would not be a priestess to the house of hours. Scorpions would grow in my head before I would simmer the early morning pump water until rust coated the teapot like blood. I would not scrape or slice or stitch. Forget my rural heritage: the dun slither of routine—homemade casseroles and biscuits, hearts swelling with ample kindness. No! No mops like disheveled women. No pails, bowls, basins. Floors clear as a pill. I was not a suckling to purity. I would not search for my reflection in a coffee table, do lugubrious errands, smell like lemons and paste. Twitch of nerve and muscle, the lamb could perish in the field, the dove and bindweed rise and freeze. But I was also lonely in the sweet prison of my body, so I let love come along and teach me otherwise.

What did I know about men as a girl? A portend: in the middle of my maternal ranch, halfway up the dizzying trail, was a secret box nailed to a tree, and when you pulled up the lid, there was a map of the land with words like Suicide, Little Pond, Four Corners known as Cachetta. What startled me most was not the enormity of my mother's land, but the pictures that framed the map—nasty pictures cut carefully and pasted so that cocks went into cunts, women's mouths were sucking their own breasts, women were on all fours like crouching begging animals, shot animals. There was a big picture of a fat woman with her fat legs spread, her breasts like gourds, her gut heavy as if pregnant; and this woman's hair was unbrushed and she was ugly, she was laughing, her cunt so small you could hardly see it, like a squirrel's hole, something you could trip into. I looked at the pictures of cocks, cocks like slugs, shrugging cocks like when you put salt on a slug and it curls, and I felt sick at the whole lot. I felt sick looking at the fat lady who got the hunters this far. She should have been ashamed of her place in the box. I imagined the men staring at her with their rifles hunched on their shoulders, spitting at her, and taking a nip, and then I imagined them squashing a cigar on her buttocks, her face. I told myself I would not be a woman, a laughingstock doomed to live life in a box.

Eros bore me away from long afternoons in stuffy fields, pledged to slake my desire. I believed at night under the dark cloth that the words whispered were sacred; I read his flesh like a religion, the customary devotion, the bride's bread and the husband's . . . I lay trusting while the world above me screamed like an envious sister. Eros had its drug-rush tactics and took me to Sparks, Nevada. Eros drove into the gated trailer park, a different type of ranch, a ranch for pleasure. I sat in the heat of the Volvo with its red pink seats, with its steering wheel big as an orb. I sat behind it and saw through it as Eros walked right through the cacti, the broken bushes and knocked at the door. I heard the whistles and laughter come from the windows. Eros tried to wave me in. Eros wanted me to watch, but I stayed in the car, thought I was safe, that playful Eros would just get a drink and look around. I thought it was fine because most wives knew this, like going out for coffee in the late afternoon. Didn't they? I was proud as Eros and the prostitute stared at me through the glass. I thought Eros wouldn't go through with it. But that time was about the only time he didn't. Eros taught me about chicken ranches, about strip joints, about pornography and dirty movies; taught me that if I wanted him, I didn't have a choice. Then my belly swelled. I metamorphosed like a god. I ate imagining the stalk joining the yolk sac, the future spine thickening, the tail bending and breaking off. Food was my only duty. I was sister to the milk cow and slopped hog. I pulled a new language from inside my uterus: *corpus luteum,* ripening follicle, tough plug of mucus. I ate thinking of my shimmering placenta, my maternal blood, those dark passages becoming bone. There were shifts in me and migrations. I ate as if waiting for my own sweet air.

How many layers did they have to get through, how many walls to get to the core where the child waited in his sacristy of blood and water, waiting dependable as Mary? I remember so little when they paralyzed my lower body, made me half-spirit, when they shaved me pre-pubescent, dipped the sponge in the red liquid and iodined my belly like a schoolgirl who skins her knee in the schoolyard. They held the dark cloth in front of me like a shroud. I could not see, split, I was purblind as they were cutting. I was the original assistant stuffed in the magician's box. I trusted I would not be injured, would come out alive, whole, stand up and walk off like Lazarus. I felt the tugs as the knife went in gentle as foreplay as when Eros patted me, pressed me down as if to shape me, mold me. Then I felt the bigger tugs, twists, as above the curtain the boy came—bright, pensive-eyed, territorial—and then his brother pearl-white, quiet, almost complacent. These two followed a year later by another who would want me, divide me.

Eros continued his pre-birth routine while I stayed faithful, became a housewife, a nurturer. Catholic, I envied the women who made love without worry, who were through with conception and birth, their fertility sealed, the tied ends of their tubes like birth-knots on the tips of children's balloons. How happy they seemed, light as helium, knowing freedom. They did not look at their wounds in the shower. Their bodies were theirs, taut-edged and accurate. Their faces guileless, safe. How stiff I became as a mother, lying down at night, feeling the imaginary child kick with its legs of a foal. How could I let it happen again? The tiny accident I feared like losing one's brakes. Reluctant grownup, I became cold.

My sons, my loves, molded me from the inside out the way man will bore through heavy winter. They stretched and flexed their limbs against my ribs the way lava works and turns inside a cone. It was as if a fiery rain shored them over onto me. I would learn to pin their hands, tameless and happy, back into blankets like clipping the wings of powerful birds. Then they grew up, became animals, pulled at each other, seized each other's neck, as if to cut it off, called each other *ho, bitch, pussy.* They shamed each other with blows and blames, slang and rancor. My sharp-edged *don't say that* went nowhere. I wanted my milk to piece them together. I wanted to be that bottomless spring, that well of buoyancy. I wrote benign words on their foreheads, scribbled nouns and adjectives as if this could save them. They shuddered, pushed me away, bobbing for breath. I was female to them, and thus invisible.

I endure with my predatory heart. Scent of death and old ash. Thirsty turn of the mirror turning mirror. Sacrificial greedy parts of the tall onyx sunflower. The morning hoarfrost rattles. I am tender and dangerous. I watch the creek water advance in its jacket of slime. What is it to *heal?* No clutter in the kitchen, nothing to be deticked, dewormed, fed, nurtured. The buds sprout fierce. Maybe the ringdoves when they coo tell of a ripening that is right, that spastic flock of rebel benediction endless in the dawn light breaking, their lingering blue sighs of a fresh measureless future, what I haven't wanted to know in my accustomed world, always conceding to the masculine handgrip. I think what the doves say is "otherwise," meaning enter the inexhaustible "whatever else" whistling in shadow, crisp bristle of wind leaping like flame.

And so what if ancestral duty clings close like a bride? So what if you have slept years in that melancholic chore of early romance? No more elixirs or new diagnosis. See what kind of noise disturbs the puffed-up universe, no matter the residual roar. Say goodbye to the numbed drugged tongue, the playhouse adage of "leave your shoes on the porch." The doves provide a counterpoint to the manic hurrah of science and theory. A rising here, there, nowhere revelation of unimaginable surprise.

Lying to God

Donna J. Gelagotis Lee

Aunt T. said it didn't matter
      that I was divorced and hadn't
      been to church in over twenty years—

nor was I going to join, even after
      I became godmother. And now the priest
      was coming to the buffet breakfast,

the priest who would *know* just by looking
      at me. What would I say if he asked me
      about the husband he thought I had?

Our Father Who?

Carol Cooley

A long black asphalt road led to St. Michaels. Stone walls were separated by stained glass, strength and story mingling effortlessly. Inviting arches lined the walkways, protective and sturdy like God's house should be. Men walked at ease here, not like alcoholic husbands. They wore all black, the color that hides stains, except for a small white spot on the throat where they express themselves. Important concepts lived here: repressed desire, humility, and clear directions to sit, stand, and kneel. Routine seemed to settle chaos. There were straight lines of hard pews with straight hard backs. A place to slouch or grieve was not the purpose for the wooden benches. They were for listening and being protected, which was why I turned to St. Michaels. I needed to be protected and taken in, like a wounded stray. I wanted God's strong masculine hand to support me and fix my broken life.

Sunday after Sunday I sat upright with strangers, all who, I was convinced, had better lives, if not more righteous lives, than I did. They were families of four, five, or six, not a family of two with a sinner single mom running the household. I sat in church as consistently as the ritual of mass, feeling undeserving of the people of St. Michaels and even God Himself. To further my feelings of impurity, until my marriage was annulled I was not allowed to participate in the Eucharistic Sacrament, the Body of Christ.

So, when it was my turn to rise, leave my straight back pew, and walk the straight line to Jesus with hands humbly folded, I stayed in my place for all to see—the woman on the pew with a toddler who cannot take in the body of Christ because she sinned. I had broken the Sacrament of Marriage, as defined by the church, and the reasons I made that choice weren't important. Repentance was important and believing this was the self punishment I chose.

In some ways going back to the Catholic church after a divorce was like going home to my parents—showing up with heavy suitcases, unsure of my reception, and asking if I could stay in my childhood room until I healed. Then, my Dad saying, "You can stay here, but you have to live by our rules," while my mother stood slightly behind him nodding her head in agreement. Then, in my beat-down, emotionally flat, and soul-deflated state of being I said, "Okay," and lugged my son and baggage upstairs, while my parents shook their heads at my mistake. In St. Michaels, I lived by His rules—the God referred throughout the bible as "He" and by the rules created by the Patriarch, the Pope, and the Priests. The rules told me that if I submitted long and hard enough, God would reward me with a taste of His goodness and protect me from Hell.

Days and weeks passed. I was grieving less, looking more at my part in the failure of the marriage, and embracing my life and role as a mother. I was thinking less like a victim and consequently more like an adult. I was healing outside of the church and as my strength was returning, I felt more restless about St. Michaels and the messages I was subjecting myself to. I wondered who could've created a rule that the divorced be deprived the symbol of Jesus's love in the spirit of church community? Certainly not a woman in a loveless marriage, where lies and spiced rum took precedence over friendship and parenting. I decided that it was a choice to believe I could not participate in the Eucharist like the other men and women. So, one Sunday while attending mass alone, I stood up like the others and moved slowly toward the redemption Jesus promised to all of us. When I arrived at the altar I looked deeply into the priest's eyes. "The Body of Christ," he said, as he held the round wafer eye level between us. "Amen," I said, as I stretched out my arms, left palm resting on top of the right, creating a bowl for his offering. The priest gently placed the host in my left hand. As I walked back to my seat, I picked up the Body of Christ, opened my mouth, and put the thin disc on my tongue. Even the image of Christ's suffering could not distract me from how stale and flavorless it tasted. I savored it, though. I allowed the host to dissolve slowly in my mouth and eventually swallowed the remains of my secret. On my knees, I was quite certain I was not the only one that day to sneak Christ's love, a long road from believing I was the only one in mass who was a sinner.

I continued to steal a Holy Communion with Jesus behind the Priest's back. Eventually, the pretend relationship I was having with Jesus's nurturing was hurting me more than it was helping. *Why am I enabling this harmful standard?* I asked myself. A more honest step toward living by the rules was to see about an annulment. So, I contacted the parish office and inquired about coming in to talk with someone about my situation. The woman on the phone gave me the office hours and said I could come in and pick up an application. "No meeting?" I asked. "For what?" she answered. I didn't know how to answer her, so I thanked her, and we hung up.

I was nervous the morning I pulled into the parish parking lot at St. Michaels. I parked the car, took my son out of his car seat, and walked to the entrance. The office resembled one you might see at a school or other institution. There were only women, southern women, working behind the desks and scurrying around doing various types of administrative duties, like filing or answering phones. I walked to the L-shaped desk and on its flat surface noticed flyers and pamphlets for marriage classes, preschool education using Christian principles, and a divorce support group. *That's interesting,* I recall thinking. *I wonder if the group helps you understand why you need to wait for Christ's love during a time when you need it the most.* A woman roughly in her early thirties, like me, came over to greet me. I was holding my son on my right side, his diapered bottom sitting securely on the top of my pelvic ridge. My hair was in a pony tail and I was wearing a T-shirt and blue jeans.

"Can I help you?" she asked in a strong southern accent, dragging the "u" a bit longer than my Pennsylvania roots were accustomed to.

"I'm here to see about an annulment," I said.

"Well, are you divorced yet?" she asked, using a long "I" when she said "divorced."

"Yes," I answered.

"What you need to do is fill out an application, send in the fee, and mail it to the address listed," she instructed.

"Then what?"

"Then it gets reviewed," she said.

"Who reviews it?" I asked.

"The Diocese reviews it. Someone at the Diocese," she said.

"How long does it take?" I asked, sensing she was getting perturbed with my questions.

"It can take about a year," she said.

"What!" I said, raising my voice.

Looking in her eyes, I knew she could not relate to the struggles I had at St. Michaels over those past several months. The only way she would ever understand is if she went through the injustice herself, and I would never wish that on her. She was in a role, doing her job, and playing by the rules of her father's house.

"So, let me get this straight," I said. "In order for me to get an annulment I need to fill out an application which gets reviewed by someone who will never meet me. From there, I must wait one year to get an answer as to whether or not I am deemed worthy in the eyes of the church and God, AND I have to pay someone to do this?"

"Do you want an application or not?" she calmly asked.

I turned around, opened the door, and left the parish office. That morning was the first time I left St. Michaels and did not hold back my tears. My son was twisting my ponytail, shooting out words from his one syllable collection, "car," "dog," and "big." I wanted to teach him a sentence, "God is not in the Catholic church," but I didn't. I strapped my son in his car seat, smiled at him, and handed him a sippy cup full of milk. He smiled back just before he pulled the cup to his mouth. I leaned my back against the car and faced St. Michaels, thinking the "Our Father" prayer should be a question and end after "who." *Our Father Who? Who is He? Where is He?* I wondered. Looking at the church, I stared at a huge structure made of stone and brick, but could no longer see a symbol of strength or a metaphor for protection, just a cement shell that will not be exempt from the pounding of storms and winds as crazy as the process of getting an annulment.

Four years passed before I walked into a Catholic church again. The occasion wasn't to be rescued, protected, or to follow the rules of a male parental God, but to tour the great St. Patrick's Cathedral in Dublin, Ireland. The church can boast over eight hundred years of worship and services. I wondered how many women over the course of that many years sat on straight back benches and denied themselves the Eucharist or felt a spiritual angst as the church's teachings separated them from a Divine Feminine spirit equal to His Almighty. How many of them had the courage to steal a nibble of Christ's Light? Had they contemplated, as I had, the irony of the crucifixion while being deemed inferior?

I entered the Roman Catholic Church that day labeled a "visitor," not a woman or someone who broke the Sacrament of Marriage. When I walked through the doors, my senses were calm and present. I absorbed all that was warm and familiar to me—the sounds of grand tolling bells, fragrant scents from lit candles, clicking heels on tile floors, and the flickering light from a collection of dancing flames praying for souls everywhere. I thought about the elderly nuns I had known when I was younger, their smiles subtle and tender. I yearned for the ritual of mass and to hear the deep bass tones in a priest's prayerful song. I wanted to dip in, just briefly this time, to taste a masculine *and* feminine spirit present in every church where humanity draws together to connect with the higher self.

Mass Revolt

Catherine McGuire

The day of the rebellion—
sitting on an attic stair, facing
his white, livid face, the rage
that seeped up from his Sunday collar,
just barely held—in truth, I was scared.
That morning had begun as others,
with the sleep-stunted motions toward church:
find the fancy garb, shiny shoes, missals,
veils—the family in a murmured swirl
along the hall, inching toward the appointed hour.
With Lucifer's own dread defiance, I sat
trembling but firm, ready to flee to attic burrows
if it came to blows. "I will not go."
"Not go?!" His face turned white, then red—
who had been so amused by mother's fear
that I would bed the first college man
I met. But now the real taboo is crossed—
no church, no god—no child of his
would take that path and live with him!
The fledging now complete and
I emerged a swan in duckling brood.
In thunderous tones he banished me—

"to church or street." And I, of course,
like passive rock refused them both
but haunched on my principles, reminded him
he'd taught me honesty, and zeal;
inquiring mind I got from him—
should I be false? Hoisted,
it seemed on his own petard, he left
telling me to "think it over." And so
the crisis passed; Sundays flowed
around my seedling doubt; a weed endured
in orthodoxy's lawn. And decades hence,
I watched his passing; wondered if my protest
had touched his deepest heresy, the root of
the despair that spread like cancer in his bones.

Hunger*

Kari Ann Owen

Time: the early 1960s.
Place: Brooklyn, New York. The entryway of Margaret's house.
Margaret is an Irish American woman in her fifties.

Welcome, missus, and welcome to your daughters . . .
oh, they're in school? Would you like to come in? It's
a bit cool here in the parlor, but the kitchen's warm as
a cow's udder . . . No? Is it cold enough out there for
fur? That stole is beautiful . . . No, you don't owe any
apology for the girls; your older one's not imposing.
We bake once a week for the whole family, and there
used to be ten of us. Begging your pardon, missus,
but . . . why is the child hungry? Because she's fat? No,
I'd sooner understand the mind of Winston Churchill.
But you don't want me to feed her. So making her
hungry will make her less fat?

---

*"Hunger" and "Angels" by Kari Ann Owen are from "Modern Life," which
is a large and open-ended series of monologues and one-act plays comprising
a wide variety of themes, from the Cuban Missile Crisis to Owen's recent
play entitled "Bernie Madoff in Hell." Sister Margaret is the same character
in both plays, forty years apart, and both "Hunger" and "Angels" take place
in the same house in Brooklyn, New York.

No (*Laughing while she knows the woman may be insane*), I'm not trying to make her fatter to spite you because you're not of our faith. And I'm not trying to bribe her to be a Catholic. She eats the gingerbread—would you like some? No? She eats it politely, no, not like a waffling pig—and she sees the beads and wants to pray the Rosary. Maybe she thinks the food comes from the Blessed Mother. But you know, missus, it's really not an imposition, so if she's hungry you may as well send her over. Coming on the sly is a little silly now that everybody knows . . . Whom did I tell? My brother the priest and my dear sister also live here. But you needn't worry; there's always enough to feed someone hungry and I don't want your money for the food.

I said I don't want your money. I do want you to feed the child, and the other child . . . never eats anything but wants to talk . . . About Ireland. She dreams of Ireland, so with that little horsie pin she wears, I tell her about the big red horses stomping their feet and raising fire along the green as they climb to heaven. You might tell her a few dreams, too . . . You tell her to quit bothering the neighbors? Am I bothering you now? Well, I hope I am, because this is America and there are laws against starving the children . . . Yes, even if your husband's a doctor with patients coming to the house like penitents to God. Or fools to the smiling thief who gives whilst he takes, takes whilst he gives.

(*Pause*)

We'll ask my brother who the police will believe, since most of them are still Irish. And you go ask your husband about hunger. And fat: it's the body feeding on itself, like you're feeding on the pain of those children, you bloody she-devil. Sure and goodbye and may Jesus save you and your children . . . I frightened you, did I? Am I really going to call the police? Keep your bloody stole.

You're afraid your husband's patients will go else-where? (*She laughs*) That'll quieten the streets after-noons . . . But can you tell me, missus, why does the fat frighten you so much? 'Cause some devil-hearted brats call them ugly? You should have grown up in Ireland; fat meant you had enough, and if you had enough you shared it, if you were Irish. We were all thin kids, and some of us were sickly, but none of us went begging to the neighbors. The neighbors came to us. So did the British, to send food out of the country.

(*Short pause*)

You're sorry. Sorry for what? Would you take some gingerbread, missus? Since you have to leave and your kids are hungry, I couldn't have you leave without something. And send them over, send them anytime.

(*As the door closes*)

You might come yourself, it looks like. Girdle peek-ing out your waistband, hair curled like iron, nothing allowed to slip but your eyes, missus . . . I . . . know those eyes; we all had eyes like that. When there was never enough. But this is America. No one has to be hungry, so the Kennedys say.

(*Calling after her*)

You can come back and sit in the kitchen if you wish, missus; there's not a chair in this house that's dirty and would harm your stole. Please don't leave without something for the children and yourself. You don't have to be hungry. This is America.

FADE TO BLACK

Angels

Time: the early 2000s.
Place: Brooklyn, New York. Margaret's house.
Sister Margaret is on her deathbed in her room at home, or in her parlor. Jesus's sister Jesse comes running in. She is young, wearing jeans and a T-shirt with a denim jacket.

JESSE: Am I late? Am I late? I'm so sorry; I'm so . . . sorry—

MARGARET: You're almost late, but I'll forgive you. Even home-care nurses are often late nowadays.

JESSE: That's mighty nice, your forgiving me.

MARGARET: You're new on this job, aren't you?

JESSE: Just flew in from Texas. I was doing rodeo duty. Those big men sure can ride. (*Jesse shakes some dust from her hair.*) May I wash up? I feel really grungy. (*Sister Margaret coughs and chokes, and Jesse helps her sit up and take a drink of water.*) I guess there isn't time . . . please don't tell my brother. About the dust.

MARGARET: I can barely talk, and anyway I don't tattle. Never did as a girl, never will as a woman.

JESSE: Me, neither.

MARGARET: So why did you fly all the way into New York?

JESSE: My brother asked me to. I get the special cases.

MARGARET: Special?

JESSE: The saintly ones.

(*Sister Margaret laughs.*)

MARGARET: Your brother's playing a joke.

JESSE: Oh, no. He almost never jokes with the dying.

MARGARET (*Pausing*): At least you're not trying to fool an old woman. (*Pause*) Irish don't die; we just get greener. So what was the joke?

JESSE: Some prominent McCarthyite lawyer who persecuted gays came down with AIDS. And my monologue about it was the last thing he watched on TV. I've got some great connections in the industry, and sometimes they play tricks for me.

MARGARET: Tricks?

JESSE: Just to get people's attention.

MARGARET: Like calling me a saint?

JESSE: We're pretty good at finding the real saints. As opposed to those overdressed demagogues who just talk.

MARGARET: That's why I stopped watching television. Before I got this lung disease . . .

JESSE: It's not just a disease now . . .

MARGARET: I know. I'm going home. To my dear sisters and brothers, my mother, father . . . Is Fr. Ryle here?

JESSE: He's already given you the Last Rites. The rest is up to us.

MARGARET: Who are you?

JESSE: You've known my brother all your life and you don't even suspect me?

MARGARET: Suspect you of what?

JESSE: It must be the clothes. Everyone thinks we wear white robes or something. How retro—

MARGARET: Don't tell me—

JESSE: Faith and appearances don't always harmonize.

MARGARET: You're—

JESSE: His sister. My brother's busy with the other twelve apostles and the NBA. If I could just get a bath and change my clothes? There's a concert at Lincoln Center. That Lennie Bernstein—

MARGARET: He always stayed a boy, with his wonder of flying wide-hearted through this poor world. Excuse me?

JESSE: Is that what you'd like to do when you get home? Hear some music? Fly with the notes through an unsoiled sky? Start thinking about it, because there isn't much time—

MARGARET: Who are you?

JESSE: It's me. Jesus's sister, Jesse. Really.

MARGARET: Dear God, I'm finally alone with an angel . . . If you're . . . Jesus's sister, don't you have all the time in the world?

JESSE: Not with this population explosion, and all the dying needing guidance to heaven—

MARGARET: Why can't you try some guidance while they're here?

JESSE: Are you angry with my family?

(*Margaret is silent. Then she takes upo an old newspaper and throws it at Jesse.*)

JESSE: Hey!

MARGARET (*Sitting up*): Who needs hell with this?

JESSE: With what?

MARGARET (*Pointing to a story in the newspaper*): They finally arrested the parents of my little neighbors, who wouldn't feed the older girl. And thirty years later . . . (*Jesse weeps*) in the same newspaper, and in the Boston newspapers and even in Ireland, young kids now grown up are telling horror tales about . . . about priests. Priests!

JESSE: They call themselves priests.

MARGARET: With vows to Jesus?

JESSE: It was just a mask for them.

MARGARET: Didn't they know they'd be found out?

JESSE: By whom? Kids can't describe such things. By the time they learn, it's often too late. That's why we needed you here—

MARGARET: But I was neither mother nor teacher—

JESSE: Oh, no. You were both, and always.

MARGARET: But I just gave them gingerbread and talked about Ireland. They needed so much more, and why didn't you stop the bloody parents?

JESSE: We're like you; we tend to trust people. Because we love them.

MARGARET: That will wear out.

JESSE: Not if you're like us.

MARGARET: If I were divine and powerful, those priests and parents would have gone to hell.

JESSE: Margaret, the good people are angry. And they have the power to change things here. Where we're going—

MARGARET: I don't know if I'm ready to go with you.

JESSE: No one's ever ready.

MARGARET: I've been praying all my life, and you're not watching out for the children.

JESSE: Margaret, Margaret, if you remember, when Jesus and I were born Herod wanted to kill all the

Jewish kids under three. Father couldn't have stopped Herod, because of the bargain. The deal.

MARGARET: What deal? Don't tell me it's Las Vegas up there.

JESSE: We give you freedom and if you need our help, you ask. We all have to choose what we really value . . . Herod chose absolute power.

MARGARET: Over children?

JESSE: We're not General Motors; we can't make people according to rigid specifications, and we don't have a quality control department.

MARGARET: Maybe you should.

JESSE: Like Hitler's? Like Herod's?

MARGARET: The nuns used to whack my fingers with a ruler when I argued like this.

JESSE: I'm sorry. They were stupid.

MARGARET: Wrong, stupid, and cruel.

JESSE: Margaret, please don't be angry at me.

MARGARET: Don't tell me I hurt your feelings.

JESSE (*Pausing*): Sure it hurts. A few power-mad lunatics terrorize the world or a neighborhood or a child, and who gets blamed? It's like losing a friend. A million friends a day, because of the speed truth travels: newspapers, radio, television. Blaming us is . . . evading responsibility for what people can do, if they're willing to do it.

MARGARET: Now listen: I fed those children, and my brother went to the police.

JESSE: But your parents let nuns beat your hands for speaking your mind. Where were the parents in all this?

MARGARET: You don't understand. We were raised to believe adults were near God. Criticizing them was . . . unthinkable blasphemy.

JESSE: If my brother had lived long enough to marry and have kids, he would put anyone in jail who laid a hand on his child.

MARGARET: My parents believed if you were whacked at school by a teacher, you deserved a good hiding at home.

JESSE: Did my father ever say that was right? Or my brother, while he was here?

MARGARET: No.

JESSE: So whose great idea was that?

MARGARET: I don't know. But I wish you could have struck that nun with lightning.

JESSE: We depend on you for action. You depend on us for knowing deeply what the right action is. Like that special voice telling you to protect those children.

MARGARET: It usually has a brogue. (*Short pause*) What else could I have done for the children?

JESSE (*Pausing*): Nothing. (*Short pause*) You saved two lives. That's why we have a special place for you.

MARGARET: Do I really deserve it?

JESSE: Lots of people do. You especially. Margaret, we're very proud of you. Thank you.

MARGARET (*Getting tired*): I never felt particularly proud, except . . . looking in that child's eyes when we talked about Ireland and the horses. She'd go from dead to living.

JESSE: She's still living. In fact, she's a riding instructor for the handicapped.

MARGARET: Is she now?

JESSE: With her own horse. And her weight is normal, and she's married, and happily. Children adore her. You passed it on.

(*Pause. Jesse stands.*)

MARGARET: Will I sit at my mother's table? Corn beef and cabbage, soda bread? Fiddling in the distance?

JESSE: Fiddling and dancing and the high flute. Neither the guns of the British nor the IRA, and never another famine. Nor being packed like parcels in the hold of a ship on your way to an unknown country.

MARGARET: And the children? I won't go without the children.

JESSE: The children are on high horses, jumping walls greater than Connemara.

MARGARET: But the ones still down here—

JESSE: You'll be watching over them and listening. You'll spend the goodness you would have spent on Earth.

MARGARET: I might get to forgive . . . forgive me, Jesse, they're like snakes eating my heart—

JESSE: Herod ate at my heart a long time, too. But once you're out of their reach, you see . . . lonely bullies weeping and peeking behind masks. Wait and see what happens when no one can be hurt by them, and they're alone.

MARGARET (*Beginning to weep*): That's hell. And they being at heart stupid little children. And they all come to you?

JESSE: Some come to us. Some don't.

MARGARET (*Weeping*): I'll finally be stepping away from them?

JESSE: The meal's waiting. (*As she fades Jesse covers her.*) But don't leave. It hurts too much without you here. Because they're still killing the children, so, Father, must we only wait for a few saints to take on the wrath of the world and speak? I want (*Flinging Sister Margaret's newspaper*) lightning and thunder and mad horses trampling the destroyers! But this isn't *The Ten Commandments*. This isn't even *Law and Order*. Sister Margaret, thank you for . . . the one child with the proud, high head. Go now to the Father and ask him who should we pray to. To stop the sexual eating of human souls! Where are the human voices? (*Turning on the radio to the musical prologue to* West Side Story) Thank you, Maestro. For making those lost kids real . . . "West Side Story." Or "Bog Side Story." Or Baghdad . . . So many kids' stories. (*As the lights fade*) Hang with me,

Lennie! (*Looking in the mirror*) Got just enough time to get presentable. (*Putting a formal shirt on over her T shirt*) Think I'll fit in? If it's black tie?

FADE TO BLACK

Confessions of a (Catholic) Presbyterian Woman

Madeleine Mysko

Late in the evening on Holy Saturday, deep in the hall closet, I find a plain white linen tablecloth that once belonged to my mother-in-law, June. I unfold the cloth and let the length of it hang from my hands.

I'm thinking, as I stand in the dim light of the hallway, about the last time I saw June in the Alzheimer's unit, and how a smile stretched across her small, pinched face when she saw me coming toward her in the recreation room. Though she had months ago lost the ability to recall my name, I could tell she was glad I'd come. And though she may have forgotten I had divorced her son (June is technically my *former* mother-in-law), I could tell she hadn't forgotten there was a sadness to be borne between us. The smile was June's best effort to make do and hold on.

The tablecloth is old, the fabric thinned to the softness of baby clothes. I remember that it belonged first to June's mother. I decide it is indeed the right cloth for my purposes, and I carry it to the ironing board.

The ironing board is set up in front of the window, in the bedroom that faces the street. The shades haven't been drawn, and it occurs to me that neighbors walking by with their dogs can look up through the dark and see me standing there, pushing the iron back and forth across yards of white. *Ironing a tablecloth for Easter,* they will think—but only if they are women of a certain age. And they will be right, though the cloth is not for the table.

I go out then into the dark, with June's old tablecloth folded over my arm, and walk the two blocks to the lot adjacent to the church. At the heart of the lot there is a labyrinth, and at the heart of the labyrinth there is a cross—rough wood pieces lashed by rope. The cross is about as tall as I am. I drape the folded length of June's tablecloth over its extended arms with the tenderness I might devote to the dressing of wounded flesh—a tenderness that startles tears to my eyes.

A car goes by, but the headlights don't reach me. It seems right that no one sees. And so I stand there a while, unable to form a single sentence of prayer, but feeling crucially centered in the sacramental, in the holy.

~

"Me? Oh, I'm a *Catholic* Presbyterian."

I've used italics for the word *Catholic*—an appeal to the ear of the reader, since it's true the emphasis falls there when I'm speaking that sentence. But in my mind, as I write it, "Catholic" is actually a parenthetical, a true modifier. On the page it is *kept,* so to speak, within bounds of the punctuation.

"(Catholic) Presbyterian." Depending upon who's asking, I may roll my eyes or smile long-sufferingly with half my mouth.

Nearly twenty years ago, when I first joined the Presbyterian Church USA, "Catholic" was my self-deprecating quip, my disclaimer (e.g.: "You want me to teach Sunday School? But I'm a *Catholic* Presbyterian. What do I know about the Bible?"). But over time I've learned that our congregation embraces a number of parenthetically Catholic Presbyterians—or I should say a number who describe themselves as "former Catholics," or who say they were "raised Catholic." It strikes me now that I have never met one who uses the term "excommunicated Catholic." I actually like the term *excommunicated* myself—for its Latinate heft, for the sharp "ex" that leaves a bitterness in the mouth, for the mournfulness of the syllables that part from communion, in order to name the banishment.

~

By accident, at the New Year's Eve party, the four of us are in the kitchen at the same time—four women of about the same age, four women who know each other mostly through various activities at church. We talk as we help ourselves to the wine, as we remove the plastic wrap from our offerings of hummus and brownies and pasta salad. Out of the blue, out of the ordinary (the usual topics of conversation, including the grown kids and the frail parents), a discovery flies up, delightful and wild: Somehow we have realized that all four of our names give requisite honor to the mother of Jesus—*Ann Maria, Mary Margaret, Judith Marie, Mary Madeleine*—and that we bear these names because all of us are *Catholic* Presbyterian women!

Oh, how this makes us laugh and fall into each other's arms and tell wild and crazy stories about our Catholic childhoods. In our silliness, we make enough noise that others come into the kitchen to see what's up.

"The four of us," Mary explains. "All named Mary or Marie."

"And Maria," Ann adds.

"Four Catholic Presbyterian women!" Judy says. This is especially funny because Judy is married to the Presbyterian minister who serves as our associate pastor.

The others don't laugh as much as we do. Still, someone thinks it would be amusing to have a picture. And so we line up with our arms around each other and smile brightly for the camera, like sorority sisters at a reunion.

A couple of days later an e-mail goes around with a photo attached: *Four (Catholic) Presbyterian Women on New Year's Eve.* Strong and accomplished women, outgoing and sometimes prophetically out*spoken* Christian women—it's such a fabulous photo that I get a peculiar feeling in my chest, a heaviness reminiscent of homesickness, though I cannot say for what.

~

I don't know what possessed my mother to return my First Communion dress to me, but I don't believe it was merely a desire to clean out her closet. At the time, I'd been married ten years and was a mother myself. At the time, my mother had for ten years been bearing the sorrow of my having married outside the Catholic Church. I was her oldest child—lovingly brought up in a Catholic home, taught by the Sisters of St. Francis all the way through high school and by the Sisters of Mercy through nursing school. This sorrow wasn't something we ever spoke about. Still, on the day my mother carried my First Communion dress back to me and hung it in my coat closet, perhaps she was still clinging to a hope. Perhaps she hoped the dress might prove to be more powerful than anything she could say.

My grandmother—my father's mother—took me to buy that dress in Hutzler's department store. I was her first grandchild, the apple of her eye, and apparently nothing would do but the finest Baltimore had to offer. Years later, long after my grandmother had died, I found it necessary to write a poem about my grandmother buying me the dress—a poem rich with details that appeal to the senses, which now seem to me heavy with nostalgia, mostly for the department store itself. There is, for example, the revolving door, inside which one would briefly be immersed in the powerful "going-round" before being deposited in "the sudden, golden dimness on the other side/ the murmur, the perfume, the occasional perfect bells."

The title of the poem is "Introit: Hutzler's, 1954." I remember reading through the entire Ordinary of the Mass, in my childhood missal, before deciding on "Introit." The imagery does indeed support a religious metaphor. And the closing lines enfold the First Communion dress itself—"inviolable organdy/ folded in tissue paper, and carried home in a Hutzler's box." Nevertheless, it makes me weak in the knees to read this poem now. It doesn't seem a religious poem at all. It just seems sentimental.

∼

We are a close family. And so, though I am no longer a practicing Catholic, I attended the Catholic weddings of my siblings and also the baptisms, First Communions, and even a few of the Confirmations of their children. I attended with joy. But always, on these joyful occasions, there was the sorrow of the Mass to be endured. For I was the member of the family who was no longer allowed to receive the sacrament of Holy Communion.

Why did it wound me so? While the rest of the family stepped into the aisle, into the line shuffling toward the rail, I would remain rigid in the pew, my head bowed over the words of the hymn—which were always about breaking bread together—and I would cry.

What was I crying about? I knew the rules of the Catholic Church, and I had broken them deliberately. To my way of thinking those rules had nothing to do with the teachings of Jesus Christ. Why not dry my tears and cast a cold eye on the empty rituals of the Roman Catholic Church? On the other hand, if the ritual could never be empty—if in fact Communion still remained for me a sacrament too holy to be taken from me (no matter what the Pope and his Canon Law might say)—why not get off my knees and just *take* it?

But of course I never took Holy Communion in the Roman Catholic Church, not in those days. Rules were rules. And I didn't want to upset my mother by committing what to her would be a sacrilege, especially not on the occasion of a wedding or a baptism or a First Holy Communion. So I stayed in the pew and cried.

～

I cannot write the poem about my First Communion dress. Instead I climb the stairs to the attic.

I find the zippered bag in which I've stored the children's clothes I cannot bring myself to give away: velvet Christmas dresses, winter coats with matching hats, all of them purchased for my children by my mother-in-law, who delighted in shopping for her grandchildren's clothes—in the best stores—as much as my grandmother did.

And there, fallen off the hanger, in the bottom of the zippered bag, is a small mound of limp and yellowed organdy. At first

I think it can't be my First Communion dress, for in my memory there is much expansiveness—puffed sleeves and a full skirt over stiff crinolines. But when I carry the limp organdy to the attic window—when I see the deep ruffles embroidered with wreaths and bows and scattered flowers, and the tiny pearl buttons down the back, and the gathered waist with the loops for the sash, which has been lost—I'm filled with the purest gratitude, that I hold in my hands what I was looking for, that my mother returned it to me so many years ago.

Standing at the attic window, in the light of evening, I bring the First Communion dress to my lips. An image comes to mind: from my childhood missal—the priest bowing toward the altar to kiss it.

I have touched my lips to a sorrow, to an old wound. I have touched my lips to the parenthetical—to what has been *kept*, what will always be kept, because it cannot be ruled away.

Blue Lights

Mary Rice

Why do you comfort, uplift me, blue lights?
Discrete cascades on the nighttime trees,
Common reminder of Christmas.

Christ. Mass time. Past time, but still not yet.
Somehow dying can't seem exploitive.
Yet why call your loving god Father?

And the dogmatic perversions of your famous mother,
impossible implosion of the awful types of male myth,
their power at once magnified and annulled:
Cyclical symbol
abstracted from the life cycle;
the body a man never touched
alike untouched by death.

Or so they would have us believe
who first erected the pedestal and its image,
lovingly caressed by their tortured minds
whose alien bodies could not touch in love.
Yet also adored by prostrate souls

wholly identified with their abused bodies
who lit other candles to the blue goddess,
drawn to the all-embracing earth mother.

Are these lights then unwitting rosaries,
magic chains to snare, becalm?
And yet—if you were only
Their quintessential myth,
why was your name
Rebellion?

Part Three

The Glorious Mysteries

Water's Wine

Allison Whittenberg

The balance of bliss is pain
The balance of pain is enlightenment
The balance of enlightenment is more enlightenment
The balance of more enlightenment is transcendence
The balance of transcendence is alienation
The balance of alienation is bliss

Exile

Colleen Shaddox

My friend tries a new church every weekend, a practice that exemplifies the virtue called hope. Nothing quite floats her spiritual boat. "They sang for forty-five minutes, then there was a reading, then we left. That's not church!" she complained. She, like me, was raised a Roman Catholic. To be raised Catholic and switch denominations is a lot like giving up Haagen-Dazs for broccoli. You miss the richness, even if you know it's bad for you.

I was about four when I acquired my taste for religion. Amid Saturday errands, Dad often stopped into the cool silence of Holy Infant Church. Lingering incense spiced the air. A single light spoke in the darkness. The candle burning by the tabernacle that held the consecrated host glowed an otherworldly red. "That light never goes out, because that's where Jesus is," my father explained. He inevitably had to drag me home to supper. I wanted to look at that light forever.

When Aunt Mae took me to a Benedictine convent to buy Mass cards, we were greeted by an old woman dressed like Mary. In a circular garden alive with color, this white-habited nun put her hand on my head and said, "God bless you, child." I could feel her stillness and her joy. "I want to be a nun!" I declared. Her eyes twinkled.

All through elementary school, I wanted to be a cloistered nun. I also wanted to marry, at various times: Michael Landon, Donny Osmond, or David Cassidy. The crushes passed. The desire to live in Christ's glow remained. The cloister's allure was heightened by family chaos. That father who so beautifully explained the Eucharist was given to drunken rages. After Mass each Sunday, jug wine propelled him into ugliness: "The Goddamned liberals are letting those welfare queens squeeze out babies and bleed taxpayers dry!" One Sunday, I objected, "Daddy, you shouldn't talk like that. Jesus was a liberal."

He sent me to my room to think about why I was wrong. Not according to the Gospels. They told me that Jesus's light shone from the oppressed as brightly as from the tabernacle. I learned then that the sacraments and the Gospels were the way to connect to God, that I couldn't take anyone else's word on spiritual matters.

In high school something happened. I began to ask questions like, "If Jesus loves the poor so much, why doesn't He give them money?" What I really wanted to know, I now believe, was, "If Jesus loves me so much, why did He give me a drunk for a father?"

I refused to go to church with my family. At school, I would sit stone-faced through prayers, testing just how little participation the Sisters of No Mercy (a pet name) would tolerate. I also raised money for refugees, collected food for pantries, and went vegetarian because livestock used up land that could have been farmed for the poor. I was a holier-than-thou unbeliever.

I grew up to be a reporter covering homeless children, prisoners, battered women. I would have sworn on a stack of Bibles that Jesus was nothing to me. But I kept a card in my wallet that said, "The truth will set you free." My newspaper launched a circulation drive in the suburbs, during which I was told to abandon my usual beat for "lite" lifestyle articles. "You're not going to write any more stories about people with AIDS," my editor said.

"That's not Christian, and I won't do it," I replied. Then I literally turned around to see who was speaking because it couldn't be me. It seems I'd gotten over Donny Osmond, but not Jesus. I suppose it wasn't so much a conversion as the end of a long period of denial.

I went to work at a soup kitchen, a Catholic one. I could be with God's poor in the kitchen then visit the sanctuary to see His light shine from the tabernacle. Heaven and Heaven. I had troubles in the decade after I returned to the Church—miscarriage, cancer, layoffs—but no longer required apologies from God.

Then my archdiocese launched a campaign against civil unions. The proposed law allowed couples to register so partners could have legal rights; no church was being asked to bless these unions. I'd always disagreed with my church about homosexuality, a subject on which Christ was mum. But now my diocese was using *the money I put in the collection plate* to oppose the civil rights of a minority.

A voice inside said: "It's not Christian, and I won't do it."

For months, I prayed for that voice to shut up. I finally got clarity when my husband asked, "If you stay, can you work to change things?"

The answer, of course, was, "No." The Catholic Church is no democracy. It's run by a select group of men who have little incentive to accommodate or even honor dissent. That is why the second largest religious group in America is so-called *lapsed Catholics*.

How I hate that phrase! As if I forgot to renew my membership! It implies a casual laziness—too *lapsed* to get out of bed Sunday mornings. There is no place I would rather be Sundays, any day, than in the presence of the Eucharist. If I could be there in good conscience, I would. My friend believes that if we keep looking we will find the faith community of our yearning. I fear that I found my one and only spiritual home at the age of four. Perhaps *exiled Catholic* is a better phrase for people like me.

If a Catholic, after prayer and study of scripture, comes to a reasoned and deeply felt conviction that differs from the hierarchy's, she ignores that experience only at the peril of ignoring God. Nothing in the current structure allows one to act on such experiences, to, as my husband put it, "work to change things." In other words, the rules we get from men trump the insights we get from God.

The wonderful thing about Catholicism is that its liturgical richness sets the stage for transcendence. As a child in that darkened church, I stared directly into the loving majesty of God. How glorious that a religion offers such profound connection to the divine. How tragic that it doesn't know enough to stop there.

Anathema

Natasha Sajé

With the judgment of the priests in their amices and albs, their
    cinctures, stoles and chasubles,
The bishops in their mitres pointing to the sky,
The rabbis in yarmulkahs and tallits, tasseled and clipped,
The saints in their garments embroidered with compass and
    square,
The ayatollahs in their black turbans and white beards,
And all the rest of the clergy
Who every day are more sure of their faith
Who every day know more of the heresies
I practice and teach—

And with the consent of the elders and of all congregations
In the presence of the Bible, the Koran, the Talmud,
In their proliferate cathedrals and cloisters,
Mosques and minarets, synagogues and temples
Etcetera etcetera and with precepts
Written herein with the curse Elisha laid upon the children and
    with all the curses
Which are written in the law and not in the law—

And through those who have endeavored by diverse threats and
    laws and promises
To take me from my way
Of living outside religion
Who raise a rod over my soul
Who will not pardon me
Whose axes ring in my flesh—

I refuse the censer and the breviary, the thurible and ciborium,
    the rosary and offertory,
I prefer my wine and bread unconsecrated, my soul unrepentant—

Cursed am I by day and cursed by night
Cursed in sleeping and cursed in waking
Cursed in going out and cursed in going in—

Let the wrath and the fury of the righteous henceforth be
    kindled against me
And lay upon me all the spells they think they can conjure—

Destroy my name under every religion and
Cut me off for my undoing from all such tribes—

So that I may live as if I am already dead.

Intersections

Lauren K. Alleyne

After Pascal

They compose us, or perhaps we house them:
We, being the junction of dust and breath;
Being, the thin line hinging consciousness

to stone. We are born the point that right runs
into accountability: counter
or concurrent. Our infant screams confirm

our options: voice or silence. The wager:
everything's at stake and so, we must choose.
If we prefer not to, then, believe this:

Faith (that rough intersection of absurd
and real) is simply hope in the chaos
that some small thing will resonate, prove us.

Like this verse, in which speech and space persist
to make meaning; where You and I connect.

Telling My Mother
I Can't Say the Rosary

Patti See

It was the UPS strike of '75, I say
pointing to the line of First Communion photos
holding up her living room.
Five sisters before me captured
in their portrait grace of Catholic girlhood
both brothers in plaid jackets and bow ties
against a starburst gray background
the girls set before the tunnel to paradise
in the same crepe paper dress and haloed veil
posed and boxed for two decades.

I wore the dress last, over my *Charlie's Angels*
tank top and running shorts in the June studio
with the borrowed prayer book and scapula
the hand-me-down rosary, my parcel

ransomed in some packed warehouse
my body not yet the Temple
my mother warned it would be
ankles crossed awaiting stigmata
that may appear, like the Holy Spirit,
at any moment. Or it was

the Lutheran convert Miss Rhinehart
who learned our prayers with us
her first-ever second grade class
accepted the alien ritual creeds, but could not
describe the wafer's sacred taste much less
name the Joyful, the Sorrowful, the Glorious.
She handed out dittoed examples of the Rosary
all winter blue bleeding to white
warning us not to sniff the fumes as we waited
for the Ugly Pickle Sucker's[1] deliverance.

Up and down tickle-belly orchard roads
we'd have surely crashed the paneled station wagon
if not for my mother's mumbling over glass beads
purer than her rounded-out trinket bought
at the *Passion Play* just past Davenport, Florida.
A knob for each decade surrounds the sterling crown
of thorns in my cupped hand, the ring topped
by the Crucifixion, on the other side tarnished
letters form *Ave Maria* with the Mother
of God assuming like mothers do.

The Evelyn Wood version, I ask
as she offers me her new treasure
compact as a travel cribbage board
more brass knuckle than absolution
more gewgaw than amulet. She slips
me the pamphlet *How to Pray the Rosary*
Cliff's notes for the religiously challenged
the Virgin Mary circled by diagrams and pagan

arrows, catechism quirky as Jumanji rules
more of the mystery we've become.

Now in my impiety I hide this promise

of redemption in my hip pocket
like an illiterate carrying Blake
what curse, what menat[2]
whatever the last little Glory be.

Notes

1. Slang for UPS drivers in elementary school circles.
2. Ring or necklace that is believed to bring divine protection

Secrets of the Confessional

Pat Montley

Sound of confessional window slamming shut and another one opening. Lights up on PRIEST standing. In front of him: WOMAN 1 kneels, facing out. At his right WOMAN 2 kneels. At his left, WOMAN 3 kneels.

WOMAN 1: Bless me, Father . . .

PRIEST: Yes, my child?

WOMAN 1: Am I your child?

PRIEST: Didn't you call me father?

WOMAN 1: Yes.

PRIEST: Well?

WOMAN 1: Well what?

PRIEST: Why did you call me father?

WOMAN 1: You told me to.

PRIEST: Do you have something to confess?

WOMAN 1: Bless me, Father, for I have sinned.

PRIEST (*Nodding*): That's it. What did you do?

WOMAN 1: I . . . I listened to the serpent.

PRIEST: Hmmm . . . what did the serpent say?

WOMAN 1: That I was smart and could think for myself.

PRIEST: And you were . . . seduced?

WOMAN 1: Yes.

PRIEST: But now you see your error and repent.

WOMAN 1: No.

PRIEST: Then what are you doing here?

WOMAN 1: I need your forgiveness.

PRIEST: Why?

WOMAN 1: To survive in the world you have created.

PRIEST: I'm afraid, my child, without repentance, you will have to . . . go to hell!

(*Sound of confessional window slamming shut, and another one opening.*)

WOMAN 2: Bless me, Father, for I have sinned.

PRIEST: Go on.

WOMAN 2: I visit the sick and try to heal them.

PRIEST: And . . . ?

WOMAN 2: Many times I've served as midwife to women giving birth.

PRIEST: Well?

WOMAN 2: I appreciate the beauty and power of nature and enjoy being a part of it.

PRIEST: Really?

WOMAN 2: I refuse to let any man control me.

PRIEST: Ah!

WOMAN 2: And for these things I am denounced as a witch.

PRIEST: So must you burn!

(*Sound of confessional window slamming shut, and another one opening.*)

WOMAN 3: Clean me, Father, for I am dirty.

PRIEST: I beg your pardon.

WOMAN 3: No. I must beg yours.

PRIEST: What is the matter?

WOMAN 3: Matter.

PRIEST: What?

WOMAN 3: I menstruate.

PRIEST: Unfortunate.

WOMAN 3: I bleed. I bloat. I expel. I make a very big mess.

PRIEST: Disgusting.

WOMAN 3: There's more.

PRIEST: Must you?

WOMAN 3: I have . . . longings . . . insatiable appetites. I want . . . I desire . . . I crave . . .

PRIEST: Sex?

WOMAN 3: Understanding. Respect. Love.

PRIEST: Liar! Repent!

WOMAN 3: No!

WOMAN 2: No!

WOMAN 1: No!

PRIEST: (*To all three*) But I could absolve you . . . in the name of the Father—

WOMAN 1: (*Interrupting*) Not anymore.

WOMAN 2: Never again.

PRIEST: I have the power.

WOMAN 3: Not if we don't give it to you.

PRIEST: What will you do?

(*Pause*)

WOMAN 1: Forgive you . . .

WOMEN 2 & 3: If you repent.

(*Sound of confessional window slamming. Blackout.*)

Note

"Secrets of the Confessional" is a scene from *Acts of Contrition* by Pat Montley, presented at the Edinburgh Fringe Festival, 2012.

Ninth Month

Leonore Wilson

I was heaven and earth then,
perfect Logos, liquid and matter,
so when the pain came
with its force of destruction
I was ready. I went into the hospital elevator
and watched the numbers rise
as if I was going to paradise.
The maternity ward was my fortress.
I could hear the lament of women,
tongues drowning as if in Hell,
but this was not,
though I was fettered
with belts and monitors, though the pangs
of labor constricted me.
Love urged me on.
In the mirror I saw myself.
I was the shape of gnosis.
I took the pain and kissed it.
I thought of the Devil taking Christ to the mountain's
pinnacle, offering him the entire world,
but no, He was born of woman,
He knew the heart's covenant,
strong-willed and determined.
He ascended into the living.

Resurrection

Mary Rice

Michelangelo drew again
and again images of the risen Christ
as a beautiful, nude man,
wholly flesh yet floating, about
to ascend to heaven and the Father.

But what the women saw
when they came to tend, as women do,
to the dead as well as the living—
what they saw
was an empty tomb
and an angel, who said, He is not
here, he is risen.

And maybe the point is
the empty tomb,
the space inside
where miracles can happen
when the stone is rolled away.

The Sentence

Leonore Wilson

And what if she had refused when the red angel came through
   the portico,
        not allowing her body to be occupied; what if she would not

be persuaded, would not offer her consent, no price would do, no
        she wanted her youth, she was just a child really, only fifteen,

she took pleasure in her flesh becoming woman, becoming desirable
        to men, she felt that desire as they stared at her breasts,

breasts unsuckled, pale doves. . . . And what if she was not persuaded
        by the lily that was held out to her, she who preferred
            small flowers,

ones that hid their beauty under shrubbery like violets or wild roses.
        She didn't want to be discovered yet, wanted to rest

in her puberty, amazed at the issue of blood that flowed from
   her monthly
        it had been only one season now and she felt both the fear

and mystery of it. . . . What if she was confused about God,
    whether he
        was she, whether motherhood meant she could no longer

touch a man not betrothed to her, how could she not when she
    loved
        so much the beckoning shape of men, that visible form

of order and awakened strength that could warm her violent idleness.
    She loved it when one would sit on the bench next to her

and she could feel his unstrung breathing want, and that to her
    was spirit.
        What if she had said no to the angel who had only one mission

to convince, what if she stood up to him, disobeyed like Eve,
    what if she had tied the knot again and prevented the
        whole world

from being saved, would we have been condemned, would God
    have looked further, or sent his son among us fully grown

so Mary could be more like us, and wouldn't we have loved her
    still because she was not immortal, she was not
        extraordinary. . . .

Interior Castle

meditation on St. Teresa

Sheila Hassell Hughes

Peter, Peter
how did you keep that woman
pumpkined-in so long?

What did she do? add a woman's touch
to the rotting shell and call it home?

Or did she carve a small space
out of her insides
a rib, perhaps, or ovary

carefully scooping the seeds
of her future, roasting and
feeding on them for strength

the wound, a tiny hollow
just big enough to squeeze
her(diminishing)self through
when you weren't looking

She must have slipped away, into her imagined and endless
country

Peter, Peter,

She dwells in crystal, a castle
her soul prismed
on the walls of the cosmos
her lover the white-hot centre light

Peter, Peter,

She is a rock
built upon

She has weathered the torrents
of sex and inquisition
growing old in her glass house of women
throwing their voices at the stones outside
and endlessly roaming
themselves

Sacrament

Donna J. Gelagotis Lee

Primal is
the urge, *primitive* is the mode of hand
to mouth—

I could love like this again and again—

this is my bread. I place my hand
on its hard crust and tear
with the other—

its aroma is all I want until

I dip into virgin oil,
touch my lips to the moist
dough—

I fork the *mizithra*
into my mouth—only to follow
with another wad of *horiatiko*

psomi. I love this life of fullness—
the ripe olive, the set
cheese, the risen dough.

Sister Ming in the
Year of the Monkey

Susan Leonardi

Though Charlie was inclined to put her down as a shrew sprouting quills and Donna to insist that she was a big bird (blue heron? scarlet ibis? white crane? Donna vacillated), Ming herself felt most like a monkey. She had, after all, been born in October, month of the monkey, 1968, year of the monkey.

And it was Spring in the following year of the monkey, 1980, that she arrived in the U.S, the departure from China sudden, rushed, and enormously puzzling. Whenever curious Ming tried to ask, her mother put her hand over her ears and yelled, "No questions!" At the other end of the journey, her father yelled worse things when he wasn't pretending not to hear her at all. As a result of such parental stonewalling, Ming never did find out (a) how her father managed to get out of China in 1971 and remain in the U.S.; (b) how her mother and father communicated—they must have, though Ming never came across letters or overheard phone calls— during his nine-year absence; or (c) who bribed what officials with how much money to facilitate the emigration of the three remaining members of the nuclear family, Mother, Ming, and Charlie.

In September Ming started school in Sacramento, St. Catherine's, sixth grade, Sister Jean Russo. Ming had at the age of three started learning English words from her next door neighbor in Shanghai, Mr. Shen. But in spite of the twenty years he had spent in Toronto before returning to his place of birth, Mr. Shen spoke with a heavy accent. Quick, clever Ming had picked it up perfectly, but Sister Jean didn't seem to appreciate Ming's mimetic genius.

Mr. Shen had a box of English books hidden in a cabinet and by the time Ming was reading Mao's Little Red Book in school, she had also figured out how to read Mr. Shen's contraband. But Sister Jean didn't know that. Sister Jean made Ming mad, always speaking to her in a loud voice, always asking her to "say that again, honey." Ming's accent faded rapidly, but Sister Jean didn't know that either, because by the end of the month, Ming—tired of repeating herself—had stopped raising her hand. Ming might have minded not being in the Lions or the Eagles, but Aurelia, who had been kind to her, was also in the lowest reading group. The Monkeys.

Once Ming had been placed in the Monkeys, Sister Jean seemed to lose what little interest in her she had. On the first library day, Sister Jean sat her down in front of the section labeled "Beginners" and pulled a thin yellow-jacketed book from the shelf. "See if you can read that," she said, "and I'll be back to check up on you."

Curious George, like Ming, was a monkey.

Curious George, like Ming, was a recent immigrant.

And what that stupid white man in the yellow hat didn't seem to know was that George, like Ming, was a girl. Ming leafed through every Curious George volume on the shelf and saw not a single indication of what she knew a boy should have. (Later Ming discovered other female Georges—first George Fayne, Nancy Drew's "boyish" friend, the only character in the series Ming liked, then George Sand, and finally George Eliot.)

By the time Sister Jean came back, Ming had read *Curious George, Curious George Gets a Medal, Curious George Rides a Bike, Curious George Takes a Job, Curious George Flies a Kite, Curious George Goes to the Hospital,* and, her favorite, *Curious George*

Learns the Alphabet (that one, at least, had an unfamiliar word in it). But Sister Jean didn't know that, because Ming had put the books back, one by one, in alphabetical order according to the first letter of the third or fourth word, since all the titles started with "Curious George."

Ming was just about to pull the worn-out, paperbound copy of *To Kill a Mockingbird* (goodbye gift from old Mr. Shen) out of her bookbag, when Sister Jean came back. "Did you read *Curious George?*" she asked.

"Yes," Ming said.

"Did you like it?"

"Yes."

"Did you learn any new words?"

"Yes."

"What were they?"

"Iguana. Just iguana."

Ming was surprised that Curious George was so much like the Chinese monkey, almost as though George had been stolen from China rather than Africa, as the book claimed. But maybe monkeys, unlike people, were the same everywhere. Ming had read all about the Chinese monkey—in one of the books her father left behind when he took off for America—inquisitive, trouble-causing, restless, adventuresome, quick, clever, fun-loving, mischievous, tricky, elusive, inventive, and smart. "Inquisitive" always came first and "inquisitive" was, Ming knew, another word for curious. Ming read about the other animals in the Chinese horoscope, too, and which ones got along best with the monkey. The Rat was at the top of the list, Monkey's perfect partner. Charlie was a Rat. Therefore, Ming concluded at age eleven, there was something seriously wrong with the whole astrological system. She gave up on it then, just as her teachers (awash with enthusiasm for the Cultural Revolution, even though by that time it was clearly not working out as planned) urged her to. But she knew the monkey was part of her, even when, many years later (after she returned from China—in another year of the monkey—to a dead mother, a scolding father, a contemptuous brother, and nightmares of bleeding bodies in Tiananmen Square, one in particular, that all her healing arts had failed to bring back to life), she turned into a tiger. Not *so* surprising, given the monkey's notorious talent for metamorphosis.

Charlie stayed a Rat, though he became an American rat, quite devoid of the excellent qualities of his Chinese counterpart, like charm and generosity. But they were getting along better these days, Ming and Charlie, now that Charlie had started working full-time at the clinic. Maybe because this, too, was a year of the Monkey, and the monkey in Ming was asserting itself again.

Donna noticed it right away and smiled at her when she found Ming standing on her head in front of the chapel. The next day Teresa—current abbess of Julian Pines—commented on her voice, the voice that Ming had so carefully blended all these years with the others', so carefully that only Karen knew its firm and perfect-pitched clarity. Until now. Ming herself was surprised by it. When Anne lost her balance during morning Tai Chi, instead of correcting the position of her left foot, Ming giggled and patted Anne's butt. At breakfast she snatched the front section of the San Francisco *Chronicle* just as Beatrice was reaching for it. "I bet you don't know what today is," Ming said to the ex-abbess, now Ming's favorite human being (Sister Bette Day Vice having died in 1997).

"Yes, I do," Beatrice said. "It's the Chinese first day of spring."

"I'm impressed," Ming said, grinning. "You can have your paper back."

"I heard it on Pacifica radio yesterday," Beatrice said, already reading the headlines, "I'm a Dog."

In the next few weeks Ming exhibited the following uncharacteristic behaviors:

— somersaulting across the common room floor
— making brownies for dessert, even though it wasn't her cooking day
— dancing around Karen one night after dinner, singing "A Very Merry Un-birthday to You"

— mounting Hildegard, the abbey's broadest goat, and riding her to the goat barn for Sharon to milk

— convincing Teresa to paint a mural of green monkeys on the wall of her bedroom (to such excellent and amusing result that there were clamorings for several more murals)

— insisting that the nuns invite all the neighbors to their annual—heretofore private—Mardi Gras celebration

— saying to Jan, "Sometime, if you're interested, I'd really like to make love to you."

At the clinic she wrote "Dr. Ming Xiang in the Year of the Monkey" in Chinese characters on her examining room wall, asked her patients to sing her a favorite song while she felt pulses and scanned organs (so far, "How Do You Solve a Problem Like Maria?" was winning the most-frequently-sung contest), told the new director that he was a worse rat than Charlie and if he didn't rescind his order that she wear gloves, at least with AIDS patients ("They're the reason I'm here, Robert; they're my *friends*"), she'd quit. She supplied the waiting room with Curious George books, both her old favorites and a few from more recent decades, though she didn't like them as much.

"Ming," Charlie said, "What's up with you? Robert thinks your hormones must be wacko."

"Little brother," she said, "do you know what year this is?"

"Of course," he said, "the year of the monkey. If I hadn't known it from all the hoopla in Chinatown, I would have deduced it from your examining room art. What of it?"

"I," Ming said, "am a monkey."

He shrugged. "So? I'm a rat."

"I've been waiting all my life to hear you say that, Charlie. Can I get you to sign an affidavit to that effect, listing, while you're at it, all the Crimes Against Ming that you have committed in the thirty-odd years of your life?"

Charlie sighed. "Monkeys grasp for the moon," he muttered, one of their father's many Ming put-downs. Ming wondered if

Charlie even knew what it meant—too much striving, too little success.

Later the same day, Ming thought of bananas. Monkey food. The Curious George books were full of them. That's what I'm going to prescribe to all my patients this year, she thought. A banana a day keeps Ming at bay. I'll write that on my exam room wall. In English.

There followed one of those minor coincidences that she—during her four-year sojourn in China studying with the great masters—had learned were common to Qigong practitioners: when she got back to the monastery that night, there was a crate marked "Organic Bananas" in the kitchen. It was late, so there was no one around to ask about it. (If there had been, she could have followed the circuitous route of the fruit: on Tuesday Benjamin Franklin Yamamoto, also known as Sister Tiklaprickia, was cruising the aisles of Berkeley Bowl when he noticed the sign "Whole Crates Only $12" over what he later described as a "shitload of bananas." He bought three crates and when he got back to San Francisco, he gave a bunch of bananas, some green, some yellow, to every kid in the neighborhood and to every homeless person within two miles of the apartment he shared with his twin brother Brian, also known as Sister Kunta Delicata, and his lover, Carlos Chavez, a former almost-member of Julian Pines Abbey, now after his year's novitiate about to take vows as a Sister of Perpetual Indulgence and to take as well the name Sister Naughty Patti. Then Benjamin Franklin Yamamoto made seventeen loaves of banana bread and gave them away, too, holding back only a few for household breakfasts.

On Thursday when he set out on his morning walk with yet another huge sack of fruit, the kids were shooting each other with banana guns and the homeless folks put up their hands and shook their heads. "What do you think we are," one of them yelled at him, "monkeys"? Since Carlos had Thursday evening choir-directing duties in Angels Camp and occasionally spent the night at the monastery to avoid the long drive home in the dark, Ben suggested he take the remaining crate along as a hostess gift to the abbey kitchen. Carlos and Brian were relieved, having overheard Ben say to a friend that they'd be dining on Senegalese Banana Stew for weeks, a dish that appeared sporadically on Ben's cooking day, the recipe a vegetarian adaptation of the Senegalese Seafood Stew in *Sundays at Moosewood*; both Carlos and Brian preferred it sporadic. Actually they preferred the original version, which also had bananas but not quite so many.)

Mostly the nuns ate what they grew, so bananas were not exactly a staple of their diet. Oh, once in a while a visitor brought a bunch for her own midnight snacks and left the soft, spotted stragglers behind. But a whole crate? Ming examined them. About two-thirds were completely green, the other third various hues of greenish yellow, one bunch, at the top, quite brown. Banana muffins, she thought, a breakfast indulgence for my holy sisters.

When Anne arrived at the common house at five o'clock the next morning to grind the coffee beans and the barley, oats, corn, and brown rice for breakfast cereal, she was startled by the cinnamon and banana smell that filled the rooms. The abbey elf at work, making use of the stuff at hand, she thought. And there was so much stuff at hand this morning. ("A whole crate, Carlos?" Donna, Karen, Anne, Beatrice, and Teresa had asked, almost in unison.)

Anne's favorite fairy tale as a child had been "The Shoemaker and the Elves." Imagine waking up to find your most onerous tasks already done and done with such care and love that it took your breath away. She had cried the first time her mother read it to her. It moved her in a way that the promised princes of the other tales had not. She reverently touched the top of one of the two dozen muffins on the cutting board—not warm but close enough—and smiled in anticipation of sitting down to a cup of coffee instead of having to start the four-grain porridge, porridge (Anne thought) most certainly the daily breakfast of the shoemaker, though probably not of the elves, who seemed more inventive.

This particular elf was named Ming, Anne deduced, when she saw the note next to the muffins, a note written in Chinese characters, no translation. Ming had long been trying to convince her sisters that they should all learn Chinese. Indeed, Ming said, as the language spoken by over half the world's population, every U.S. citizen should learn it. So far, none of the nuns had (unless you counted Anne's six-week infatuation with *Chinese for Dummies*, which Ming did not).

Ming the Monkey, Anne said aloud to the empty house. Feeding us monkey food. At the clinic on Thursday nights until eight, a two-hour drive home, and then she makes muffins? What *has* gotten into that woman? Anne laughed at the prospect of Carlos facing yet another banana breakfast.

Though it was cold and dark in the Sierra foothills this February morning, by the time Anne had emptied her mug, Ming was already outside the chapel doing Five Animal Frolics in the moonlight. Anne watched the movements—some quick and bird-like, some so slow and careful that water seemed the medium in which Ming moved. Anne knew that no matter how many mornings she joined in, she'd never achieve that precision, that fluidity. But, Ming reminded her whenever Anne got discouraged, Ming had been doing Qigong since she was three and a half, only later learning, she told Anne once, that Mao had forbidden the practice and that the old woman who lifted her arms and kicked her legs behind her apartment building every morning, who let little Ming lift *her* arms and kick *her* legs in imitation, was, therefore, a dangerous outlaw.

Leaning against the chapel wall, Anne watched Ming until she heard the first of the others, soft footfalls on the dirt path, arrive for morning prayers. Anne stood up straight and headed to the small mud room that joined common house and chapel, the room in which ten white robes hung on hefty hooks, a name printed in Kathleen's calligraphic hand over each. As she dropped the Anne-robe over her head, she felt Ming come up behind her. Ming touched her shoulders and, breaking the Great Silence that the nuns observed in the reverent but casual way they observed all the monastic traditions they hadn't discarded completely, whispered (as though, Anne thought, letting go a secret whose insistent roots had just broken through its too-small pot):

"Anne, did you know that Curious George was a girl?"

Ming's Banana Muffins

Mix together:

 2 cups whole grain flours (her preferred blend: equal parts oat, barley, brown rice, and spelt)
 1 teaspoon baking soda
 1 teaspoon baking powder
 2 teaspoons ground cinnamon
 a pinch of ground cloves

Add:

 2 beaten eggs
 4 mashed ripe bananas (Usually Ming uses a cup of mashed winter squash, one or more of the many varieties that grow abundantly in the monastery garden. In that case, of course, the recipe is called "Ming's Pumpkin Muffins" or "Ming's Butternut Squash Muffins.")
 1 teaspoon vanilla
 ½ cup canola oil
 ½ cup honey (clever Ming measures the honey in the same cup she uses to measure the oil so that the honey doesn't stick)
 ⅓ cup buttermilk (Ming uses goat whey, because goats are what they've got at Julian Pines Abbey; buttermilk—non-fat, low-fat, full-fat, doesn't matter—will work as well, maybe better.)

Fold in:

 ½ cup (plus a few extra) chocolate chips—optional (Ming developed, after her naturalization hearing, a mild addiction to chocolate. How could you be an American, she asked Donna, without an addiction? Sometimes—though never in premenstrual season—Ming substitutes—or adds—pecans, raisins, or a cup of blueberries.)

Mix thoroughly and pour into oiled muffin tins. Bake for 20 minutes at 350. Should be firm to the touch or, alternatively, should pass the toothpick test. (Though there is a package—now nearly ten years old—of toothpicks in the monastery "miscellaneous" drawer, the nuns, concerned about deforestation, use them sparingly.)

Anthony's Asceticism

Ava C. Cipri

Into the desert margins (Red Sea)
a counter-world to women, where man absolves himself again

transforms through the body, a kind of stalemate,
no talk of transcendence here . . .

      only of: empty bellies   sexual renunciation
      selling wares at the market
      night's knockings of female flesh at the door

take two dried loaves
glimpse   incorporeal angels

The Taste Of Apples

Lauren K. Alleyne

These days there is speculation; they say it was not an apple Eve
    held to Adam's mouth
and ground against his teeth; it was a fig, they say,

maybe a mango, perhaps a pomegranate, a plum—fruit more
    exotic and tempting,
more worthy of the Fall. I know apples, polished

skin like blood like wine like war binding tight the white flesh,
    the black pits
pressed into the narrow center sleeping like sin like sex

like hunger. They say Paradise was tropical, filled with sultry
    days and balmy nights
too unlike the chill autumn winds needed for apples

to thrive, to come to full fruit. They say it comes down to the
    geographic impossibility.
I know apples, the way the taste of them knots

the tongue in thick accents, the sandy bite, the sharp sound of
    separation and the jagged hole
it leaves, the tempered flow of juice of tears of sweetness.

They still say that Eve should have known better, been wiser;
     should never have strayed,
or disobeyed her creator's command. But I know apples,

the way the first bite sticks in the throat, the dark rush of
     knowing, the heady flavor,
the echo of the serpent's hiss, saying *taste, taste and see.*

Paula Timpson

Unruly
is
following
Jesus
not the world
Unruly is
being truth and wishing upon
every morning sun
unruly is touching
grace
and finding meaning in the moments
surrendered to the Lord
Creator of stars and moon
children & peace—
unruly is the woman who
trusts her
inner light,
not the spotlight—

Unruly she is, free
unruly, she is, free
to be
a child of God
starry-eyed and simple,
child's mind
honoring every shooting star,

away from tv
is
the quiet heart
that shines
deep
into children's laughter and miracles
of positive
energy and
hope!
unruly is the one who turns away from
the common ways of the world into the
mirror inside
shining warm sun
forever

Unruly she begins a
turn around of souls
survivors and
heroes
learning to be capable within
themselves—
unruly she believes in the quiet power of prayer . . .
touching bare
souls
spirits
renew and stretch toward
the parallel sunset that is pink-red
trust
love

Notes on Contributors

Lauren K. Alleyne is a native of Trinidad and Tobago. She received her MFA in Creative Writing from Cornell University and is currently an assistant professor of English and poet in residence at The University of Dubuque. Her chapbook, *Dawn In The Kaatskills,* was published in April 2008 by Longshore Press.

K. Biadaszkiewicz has published fiction, poems, and theatre scripts nationally and internationally. Her plays have been produced throughout the United States and in Europe. Her work is represented in the Applause Anthology, *Best American Short Plays.* Biadaszkiewicz wrote the story "Nothing Soup" to celebrate the life of her extraordinary mother, Helenka Biadaszkiewicz.

Renée Bondy is a Canadian historian whose current research examines women religious in the Vatican II and post–Vatican II years. Her writing on contemporary feminist themes has appeared in such popular venues as *Bitch Magazine* and the Canadian feminist publication *Herizons.* She teaches in the Women's Studies Program at the University of Windsor in Ontario, Canada.

Suzanne Camino is a musician and teacher living in Ann Arbor, Michigan. Her poetry and essays have appeared in *The Spring Wind Journal, On the Edge, The Journal of the International Institute, The International Peace Update,* and on the Web site commondreams.org. She is a member of St. Leo Parish in Detroit.

Leah M. Cano is a teacher/writer living in Laguna Beach, California. She has written for *Transitions Abroad Magazine* and *MAMM Magazine*, and she has been featured in the Experiment for International Living and Vermont Studio Center Web sites. She is also a contributor to recent Chicken Soup for the Soul anthologies entitled *Tough Times, Tough People* and the upcoming *Count Your Blessings*.

Ava C. Cipri has an MFA from Syracuse University, where she served on the staff of *Salt Hill*. She teaches creative writing at Duquesne University. Recent work appears in *2River View, Drunken Boat, The Ghazal Page, NZPR,* and *WHR,* among other publications. Her award-winning Tanka Sequence "From the Barre" is featured in AHA Books' anthology *Twenty Years, Tanka Splendor*.

Sarah Elizabeth Colona lives and teaches in her home state of New Jersey. Her chapbook, *Thimbles,* was published by dancing girl press. Her first book, *Hibernaculum,* was released in March from Gold Wake Press. She is a graduate of George Mason's MFA program.

Carol Cooley received her BS and MA from Duquesne University. Her writing has been published in various journals and received Honorable Mentions from the *North Carolina Literary Review* and *Glimmer Train Press.* Married with two children, she works as a healthcare professional in North Carolina. She no longer attends church.

Jeana DelRosso is professor of English and Women's Studies and director of the Honors Program at Notre Dame of Maryland University in Baltimore. Her book, *Writing Catholic Women: Contemporary International Catholic Girlhood Narratives* (2005), and her co-edited collection, *The Catholic Church and Unruly Women Writers: Critical Essays* (2007), were published by Palgrave Macmillan. Her articles have appeared in *NWSA Journal* and *MELUS.*

Dolores DeLuise holds a PhD in English from the Graduate Center of the City University of New York. She is an associate professor of English at BMCC/CUNY, where she teaches writing and literature. Her research and scholarship are in women's literature, pedagogy, goddess studies, and creative nonfiction. She is studying southern Italian ritual tambourine and tarantella, is married, and has a grown daughter and two Chihuahuas.

Liz Dolan's first poetry collection, *They Abide,* has been published by March Street Press. A four-time Pushcart nominee, she has also received a 2009 fellowship as an established professional from the DE Division of the Arts. Her second manuscript was nominated for the Robert McGovern Prize, Ashland University.

Susanne Dutton is a former parish pastoral associate, hospital chaplain, and president of the parish professionals of the Diocese of Richmond. She currently lives in Norfolk, Virginia, serves as a mediator in the courts, and enjoys the criticism so liberally available at the Muse Writing Center.

Leigh Eicke has studied seventeenth- and eighteenth-century women's political writing, and she is co-editor of *The Catholic Church and Unruly Women Writers: Critical Essays.* She lives in Grand Rapids, Michigan, and tutors for the Literacy Center of West Michigan.

Annarose Fitzgerald is a PhD student at the University of New Mexico specializing in the uses of Catholic imagery in early modern British poetry. She has studied creative writing at Barnard College and the University of Connecticut, and she spends her time reading and writing unruly Catholic texts.

Pamela A. Galbreath holds an MFA in Creative Writing and teaches at the University of Wyoming. Her work has placed in the Wyoming Writers' and New England Writers competitions and is published in *The North American Review, The Vermont Literary Review, South Loop Review: Creative Nonfiction + Art,* and *TrailBLAZER.*

Stasha Ginsburg loves to write, travel, and teach. She rediscovered girltruth while writing a coming of age memoir, *girltruth from the belly*. Stasha has worked with youth and adults in Russia, Europe, Mexico, and the United States. Her poetry, photographs, and narrative nonfiction have been published online and in journals.

Martha K. Grant survived fifteen years of Catholic schooling. To this day she refuses to wear navy blue. Her eclectic spiritual life finds expression in both poetry and fiber art collages, and at times a combination of the two genres. She lives and works in the Texas Hill Country.

Sheila Hassell Hughes is chair of English and former director of Women's and Gender Studies at the University of Dayton. Her research addresses gender and religion in American women's writing. She has published articles and poems in journals such as *SAIL: Studies in American Indian Literatures, African American Review, American Quarterly, Religion and Literature, Literature and Theology,* and the *Lullwater Review*.

Ana Kothe is professor of Comparative Literature at the University of Puerto Rico, Mayagüez. She has published articles on issues of gender in *Modern Language Studies, English Language Notes,* and *Women's Studies.* She is co-editor of *The Catholic Church and Unruly Women Writers: Critical Essays* (Palgrave 2007) and is currently working with Stéphane Pillet on a translation of a Breton legend about an eighteenth-century female brigand.

Donna J. Gelagotis Lee's book, *On the Altar of Greece,* winner of the Gival Press Poetry Award, received an Eric Hoffer Book Award: Notable for Art Category and was nominated for a *Los Angeles Times* Book Prize. Her poetry has appeared in numerous literary and scholarly journals.

Susan Leonardi lives, cooks, and eats in Davis, California. A recovering academic, she does freelance writing, including her community newsletter, "The Covell CURmudgeon," and the wine column ("Wineaux") for *The Davis Enterprise*. Publications include *And Then They Were Nuns* (a novel), *Dangerous by Degrees,* and *The Diva's Mouth.*

Lacey Louwagie is a freelance writer and editor, feminist, and cradle Catholic. She loves exploring religion and spirituality, and she's a member of the Call to Action Young Adult Catholics blog team. She recently moved into her godmother's house in rural Minnesota and inherited an impressive collection of Virgin Mary paraphernalia.

Martha Marinara earned an MA in Creative Writing from SCSU and a PhD in Rhetoric from Lehigh University. She writes poetry and fiction, publishing recently in *Massachusetts Review, Xavier Review, FEMSPEC, Pelican Review,* and *Broken Bridge Review.* She won the 2000 Central Florida United Arts Award for poetry. Marinara's first novel, *Street Angel,* was published in 2006.

Catherine McGuire has been widely published over the past two decades, including in *The Lyric, New Verse News, The Smoking Poet, Adagio, Green Fuse, Poetry In Motion,* and *MReview.* Her chapbook, *Palimpsests,* was published by Uttered Chaos in 2011. With her new garden collection, *Glimpses of a Garden,* she has three self-published chapbooks.

Patricia Montley has an MA in theology and a PhD in theatre. She has had twelve plays published, more than 150 productions, and won or placed in more than two dozen playwriting contests. Her work has been supported by grants from state arts councils and foundations and residencies at artists' colonies. She is a member of the Dramatists Guild.

Madeleine Mysko teaches in the Advanced Academic Programs of The Johns Hopkins University. Her work has been published in journals including *The Hudson Review, Shenandoah, River Styx,* and *Bellevue Literary Review.* Her first novel, *Bringing Vincent Home* (Plain View Press, 2007) is based on her experiences as an Army nurse.

Kari Ann Owen is a scholar in religion, theology, and literature. Born Karen Iris Bogen in Brooklyn, New York, her plays have been performed at the John F. Kennedy Center for the Performing Arts during the Very Special Arts Festival in June 2004, and at the George R. Moscone Center and Fort Mason Center, San Francisco.

Mary Rice was a poet and essayist living in Cambridge, Mass. Her work appeared in a variety of publications, including *Ms., Sojourner,* and the *WHL Review.* She was an editor of *The Second Wave,* and she wrote and produced short documentaries shown on CCTV in Cambridge. Mary died on August 13, 2011.

Natasha Sajé's first book of poems, *Red Under the Skin,* won the Agnes Lynch Starrett prize and the Towson State Prize in Literature. Her second collection of poems, *Bend,* was awarded the Utah Book Award in Poetry. Her poems, reviews, and essays appear in many journals, including *The Henry James Review, Kenyon Review, New Republic, Paris Review, Parnassus, Chelsea, Gettysburg Review, Legacy: Journal of American Women Writers, Ploughshares, Pool,* and *The Writer's Chronicle.*

Patti See has published stories, poems, and essays in *Salon Magazine, Women's Studies Quarterly, Journal of Developmental Education, The Wisconsin Academy Review, The Southwest Review, HipMama, Inside HigherEd,* as well as other many magazines and anthologies. She is the co-editor of *Higher Learning: Reading and Writing About College,* published by Pearson/Prentice-Hall, and the poetry collection *Love's Bluff,* published by Plainview Press. She teaches developmental education and Women's Studies at the University of Wisconsin—Eau Claire.

Colleen Shaddox's work appears on National Public Radio and in many publications, including *The Washington Post* and *The New York Times.* In addition to her journalism, she helps nonprofits advance change through communication. She's especially committed to juvenile justice reform in Connecticut, where she lives with her husband and son.

Mary-Antoinette Smith is associate professor of eighteenth- and nineteenth-century British Literature, director of Women's Studies, and creative writer at Seattle University. She specializes in gender theory and interrogates oppressive stratifications as they are reflected in race, class, and gender issues across literary genres from 1660 to 1901.

Paula Timpson, published poetess, breathes poetry daily, including through her "Spirit" series of poetry books. Paula enjoys bringing out the best in others and sharing her art with the world through her poetry ministry; Paula brings peace and love; Paula enjoys meditation, nature, swimming, and her spirited son Jamesey and husband Jimmy.

Allison Whittenberg is a poet and novelist. Her books *Life is Fine, Sweet Thang, Hollywood and Maine,* and *Tutored,* were published by Random House. She went to grade school at St. Francis De Sales School. She lives in Philadelphia.

Leonore Wilson has taught English and Creative Writing at various colleges and universities in the San Francisco Bay Area. She is on the advisory MFA panel of St. Mary's College in Moraga, California.